Ambush at Skyline Ranch

Pinkerton Agent Cameron Scott arrives at the crossroads town of Willow Branch Creek seeking answers to a series of train robberies. He gets more than he bargained for when he befriends the lovely Becky Drake while defending her son from one of rancher Jim Gilson's cowpunchers. To complicate matters, an old enemy has come to town; Larry Strickland, who did prison time thanks to Cam, and now wants revenge. Things go from bad to worse and culminate in both a train robbery and a blazing gunfight at Skyline Ranch that forces Cam to use his hard-earned skill as a gunslinger to save not only his own life, but that of the woman he loves.

Ambush at Skyline Ranch

Thomas McNulty

A Black Horse Western

ROBERT HALE

© Thomas McNulty 2018
First published in Great Britain 2018

ISBN 978-0-7198-2856-0

The Crowood Press
The Stable Block
Crowood Lane
Ramsbury
Marlborough
Wiltshire SN8 2HR

www.bhwesterns.com

Robert Hale is an imprint
of The Crowood Press

For my beautiful wife, Jan,
our friend Joe Bonadonna,
and to the memory of
Roy Rogers and Dale Evans

ONE

Out there where the cottonwoods blow the town of Willow Branch Creek shimmered like an oasis among the tall pines and between the rolling hills of wheat and grass. It lay there gleaming in the distance like something that had been painted on a canvas and reproduced in a magazine. There was an austere beauty to the scene, which included a railroad track that had forever taken the place of the Pony Express and stagecoach lines, gone now, all of them; but even with such industrial expansion the west was still savage, lonely, and often brutal.

At sunset the trail darkened and the sky turned purple. Cameron Scott rode his Paint over a hill and paused to watch the yellow clouds melt into the lavender horizon, the sun's last rays cutting across a green sward of trees down near Willow Branch Creek. Tugging the reins, he spurred his horse off the skyline and cantered down a slope until he could hear the creek's water gently tumbling over rocks. He decided it was a good place to camp.

He was at the Kansas border, but he wasn't yet certain how far to Dodge City. The pastoral view of Willow Branch Creek and the small wooden sign that announced the city limits as five miles were enough to satisfy him. This was the town he'd been looking for. He hobbled his horse and made a fire. Camping in a grove of pines meant the smoke from his fire would dissipate as it rose into the branches. Cameron Scott was a man who had learned caution before entering a strange town. He had been in enough faraway locations to understand that patience and simple observation were assets to be nurtured.

He drank his Arbuckle's coffee black and thick from a tin cup and chewed his strips of beef jerky. He wished he had some biscuits, but tomorrow he would be able to fill up his supplies. The forest around him was quiet save for the occasional hoot of an owl. He watched the flames of his campfire lick at the deciduous branches he had piled in a circle, and when the fire had consumed most of the wood he stared sleepily at the golden embers that crackled gently in the night.

He was nearly to his chosen destination, and while the landscape was unfamiliar to him, he would venture to find his way around as swiftly as possible.

Deep in the night he awoke to a distant sound of galloping hoofs. The sound drew closer and instinctively his right hand dropped to his holster. His thumb pushed off the leather hammer loop and he rose to a squatting position. The fire had burned out and he had eased himself back on his blanket without realizing it and fallen asleep. He wondered what time it was. Carefully he stood up, shrugging off the last vestiges of sleep. A dream of a fancy girl he once danced with in a San Antonio saloon tumbled away like a leaf in a breeze.

In the morning he awoke to a paradise of rolling hills bathed in sunlight, the soft call of birds and the whisper of tall prairie grass still fresh with dew. The town of Willow Branch Creek was an easy ride and he cantered into town anticipating the whiskey he wanted to toss down his parched throat.

Willow Branch Creek was already bustling with activity. He passed a large feed and grain warehouse, two saloons, a dress shop, a church, and a general store that advertised canned goods, coffee, flour, shirts, Stetsons, boots, ammunition and dungarees. A row of new pick-axes and shovels was lined up on the boardwalk.

As he reined his horse and dismounted, a boy, tall and slender, was thrown out of the store head first. He skidded along the boardwalk, his face twisted in pain as his elbows scraped along the rough planks. Immediately behind him, a man stepped out of the store, a quirly drifting smoke from between his lips, his unshaven face glistening with sweat. Pale blue eyes squinted out from beneath the battered Stetson that was pushed back from his shining forehead, the perspiration running in rivulets down his face.

Cameron noted the low-slung holster on his right

hip and the notches in the walnut grip. He tethered his horse at the hitching post and helped the boy to his feet by hooking a hand under his arm.

'You all right, son?'

'I ain't your son!' the boy snapped. He jerked his arm free.

'Easy boy, I'm just helpin' you up.'

'He don't need help.' The man stared at him long and hard with those pale blue eyes. They were the kind of eyes a saloon girl might fancy, except the man was plain ugly and unclean in all other regards. Cameron didn't like those eyes. They were soulless, lacking in compassion. They were cold, like blue ice. The sneer on the man's face told as much about him as his unkempt appearance.

'Oh, is that right?' Cameron said. 'He looks shook up to me.' Turning to the boy he said, 'What's goin' on here?'

'It's nothing. I got let go.'

The man stepped forward and Cameron heard his spurs clanging dully. Behind him another man emerged from the saloon, an older, fat man with white hair, wearing an apron.

'Mister, this is none of your business. You best stay out of this. We don't take to strangers in town.'

Cameron faced the first man and leveled his gaze. 'We haven't been introduced. I'm Cameron Scott.' But Cameron never raised his hand to shake, rather staring coolly back at the man, who didn't flinch. In fact, something that might have been a grin creased the man's mouth as he decided to play along.

'All right then, I'm Bill Drucker.'

'What did this boy do to cause him being roughed up?'

'He's got a mouth like his father, that's what he done,' Drucker said. 'Not that it's any of your business, like I said.'

Cameron was acutely aware that Drucker had sized him up just as quickly as he had Drucker, and both had correctly estimated the other man to be trouble. All that remained was to see who would still be standing; the thought was clear in Cameron's mind and he accepted it as such, having encountered the likes of Bill Drucker many times before.

'He works for me,' the old shopkeeper said. 'He should have kept his mouth shut.'

'You stay out of this, too, Gustav,' Drucker said.

'You're done working for me, Randy,' Gustav said. 'Get on home. You can collect what wages I owe you on Friday.'

Randy had dusted himself off, his face red as a cherry. His shirt was torn at the elbow and Cameron saw blood smeared on the torn fabric. He guessed the boy was about fifteen, give or take a year.

'That ain't fair!' Randy said. 'You know my ma needs the wages I make.'

Cameron looked at Gustav. 'He got thrown real hard. That don't seem fair considering Drucker here is bigger.'

Drucker moved up swiftly next to Cameron, the

11

spurs still clanking, the quirly dropped into the dust.

'Stay out of it.'

'Listen,' Cameron said, 'I'd appreciate it if you took a step back. I've smelled hogs in a farmyard that remind me of you. As for the boy, I'm just making a friendly suggestion.'

Drucker's expression gave away the move, and as he went to throw his punch Cameron's fist smashed his nose, which sent him back a step, blood bursting from his shattered nostrils. Cameron stepped in and hit him again, this time his fist cracking loose a yellow tooth that was ejected from his mouth in a string of blood and spit. Then Cameron brought up his left fist in an uppercut that slammed the air from Drucker's lungs, and hit a right-cross down on the side of Drucker's head that put him on his knees.

'Now, don't draw your gun,' Cameron said.

Drucker was wheezing and spitting blood, his eyes welling with tears that appeared to enrage him further as he struggled with the pain that undoubtedly racked his head. When he pushed himself to his feet with his gun drawn Cameron chopped it out of his hand and kicked him square in the chest. Drucker was flung back into the dirt caterwauling like an old maid. Cameron picked up the gun and punched out the cartridges and pocketed them.

'I told you not to do that,' he said. 'I want you to understand something. This was a fair fight and we can leave it at that. But if you get any idea about coming at me again I won't hesitate to shoot. Keep that in mind.'

Cameron tossed the gun at the man's feet. Randy and Gustav were staring at him.

'This looks like a pleasant little town. Can you recommend which hotel is the cleanest?'

Gustav recovered first, stammering, 'I . . . I guess, well, the Timber Ridge Hotel gets all the railroad people.'

'Fine.' He looked at Randy. 'Nice meeting you, Randy. I'll be around a few days and if this *hombre* bothers you again, let me know.'

'I can take care of myself,' Randy said indignantly.

'I believe you,' Cameron said, 'but you have a ways to go before you can handle a hog farmer like Mister Drucker down there.'

Turning his back on them he untied his horse and led it down the street toward the Timber Ridge Hotel. He was tempted to look back but his instincts told him Drucker was down for now. Handling him later was another matter entirely.

Once again lashing the reins to a hitching post, he removed his saddle-bags and Winchester and trudged into the Timber Ridge Hotel. The lobby was far more spacious than such out-of-the-way locations usually boasted. A lot of money had been put into the hotel and for a moment he hesitated. The mahogany furniture and oil paintings of pastoral scenes made him wonder if he could afford the price of a room. The sign even bragged that a barber was available for half a dollar. A warm bath would cost a dollar, which Cameron thought was too high a price. The nearby creeks and streams were free and a man could tough out the chill and clean up fairly quickly. A dollar was exorbitant, but he supposed there were always those with money willing to pay for such comforts.

The clerk was a young man with a head full of black hair slicked down with oil. He wore a white shirt with a red bow-tie. Cameron had seen slick men like this in Denver. They were mostly harmless, although a few had an attitude of superiority that irritated him. This clerk was no exception. He peered at Cameron with distaste.

'You rode in on a horse?' the clerk asked.

'I did. That's what horses are for. How much for a room?'

'Two dollars a day, payable in advance. Most visitors come here by train. We've had fancy ladies from as far as Chicago stay here.'

'Is that so? Well, I'll stay three days. Give me a room with a soft bed that one of those fancy Chicago ladies slept in.' Cameron winked at the clerk and the young man's face turned red. He paid him in silver.

The room had a window that looked out on the street. A glance outside confirmed that Drucker had ambled away, as had the kid, Randy. Old Gustav no doubt had retreated into his shop. He draped the saddle-bags over a chair, propped the '73 Winchester next to the nightstand, and unbuckled his gunbelt. Kicking off his boots, he sat himself back on the bed with his .45 Colt single-action revolver in his right hand. The door was locked, but experience taught him that didn't matter. Drucker was bound to get worked up, although he would probably wait until a doctor had worked on his busted nose and given him some laudanum.

He still had that hankerin' for a short glass of whiskey, but fatigue had a way of creeping up on a man. He dozed lightly, enjoying the breeze that came in through the window. He did not need much rest. The soft mattress did all the work, he thought, and sure helped get the knots out of a man's back after days of following the skyline.

He rose after an hour, strapped on his gunbelt, pulled on his boots and went out looking for dinner. The late afternoon sun had slipped toward the tree-line as he made his way down the boardwalk. The sky was tinted with yellow and pink and the birds sang earnestly in the trees. The tranquility of the town of Willow Branch Creek was not lost on him. He been riding trails a long time and had stopped in a lot of towns, but so many of them were forgettable. This town was different.

He ate a steak dinner at the Grey Restaurant. The steak was served with slices of fried potato and a piece of apple pie. Two cups of strong coffee set him right. The food was good, a tad overpriced, but he could afford it. He had saved his money and wouldn't mind spending it in a nice town like Willow Branch Creek. He asked no questions and listened to whatever small tidbits of conversation he could pick up. The other patrons were dressed in clean clothes and looked like gentle people. He heard the name Gilson mentioned twice. There was no mention of his encounter with Drucker that he heard, but that didn't mean much.

He paid the bill and once more strolled the board-walk. He had several saloons to choose from. He chose the Big Elk Saloon because it rested in the center of the long street, and was closest to the rail-road depot.

The Big Elk Saloon was as spacious and comfort-able as any place in town. Although it was in many ways a typical saloon, it stood out because of its cleanliness and friendly atmosphere. The place was crowded, but there weren't the usual boisterous shouts and bawdy songs that distinguished so many western saloons. The barman wore a short string tie on the neck of his starched button-down shirt. The bowler hat and walrus mustache gave him the appearance of a cultured dandy. Still, he looked tough. There was nothing phony about the man. He stood a good six feet tall and appraised Cameron the moment he pushed through the batwing doors. Cameron took a seat on a leather-upholstered stool.

'A small glass of whiskey and a beer.'

'You're the one that had a time with Bill Drucker,' the man said. He set his hands on the bar and looked into Cameron's face.

'Word travels fast.'

'Drucker won't forget you. Put your gun on the bar. I'll give it back when you leave. If you come in here again don't be wearing it.'

'I was beginning to think this was a friendly town.'

The man moved his vest to one side to reveal the sheriff's badge pinned to his shirt. 'It is, and we'll keep it that way. Now set the gun down and you and I will get along fine. I have a shotgun down here under the bar.'

Cameron reluctantly eased his gun from the holster and set it on the bar. The gun disappeared, to be replaced by his requested whiskey and beer.

'I'm Sheriff Charlie Kerrigan.'

'Cameron Scott. Pleased to meet you.'

'Are you wanted for anything?'

'Nope. Cow punching from Texas to Oklahoma and back again. Been riding trail with some money I saved or won at poker.'

The voice that boomed across the room took both men by surprise. 'I'll vouch for this young rascal, sheriff, he's an old saddle tramp pal of mine!'

They turned and looked at the rotund man whose heavy frame belied his lightness of foot as he approached them with eyes that shone in merriment, a big smile plastered across his white-whiskered face. The ten-gallon Stetson, jangling spurs and pearl-blue silk bandanna around his neck all bespoke a traditional westerner, right down to his Texas-made cowhide boots. 'Hot damn! So Cameron Scott still walks the earth! I'll be danged! It sure is good to see you, sonny boy!'

Cameron slid off his stool and vigorously shook hands with his old friend.

'Montague Irving Gallant, you old snake charmer! I thought you had followed Custer and Hickok down the long trail!'

'Monty, you know this cowpuncher?' the sheriff asked.

'I sure do! We worked many a cattle drive together when he was just a young pup and still green as spring grass!' Monty's laughter echoed across the saloon.

'Well, your old friend here busted up Bill Drucker earlier today.'

Monty raised a quizzical eyebrow and considered Cameron with a twinkle in his eye. 'Is that so? Well, all the more reason to celebrate this reunion. Drucker had it coming one way or another. Now, c'mon and sit over here at my table and let's get the lowdown. Fetch those beers over here will you, Sheriff?'

With their drinks in front of them, Cameron and Monty Gallant set to the work of imbibing them together. After a few beers they were reminiscing about a cattle drive near the Red River and the dog-faced woman that served them cold beans on rainy nights; the dancing *senoritas* of San Antonio, and the boys with cow pies for brains that nearly ruined many a round-up.

'So how did you end up here?' Cameron finally asked.

'I work as a carpenter and help the old Swede, Ernst, with blacksmithing. It was time.' Monty took a long gulp of beer and wiped the foam from his whiskers with his sleeve. 'You know how it is. A man that rides alone across the prairie and through the tall forests is a man that understands loneliness. And he's a man that can get lost in a saloon girl's eyes and mistake it for love, just like I have. A whiskey bottle helps that along. It's those long nights under the pines or on a mountain switchback, all huddled up in a Mexican blanket as that lonely wind blows through the canyons.'

He paused, his eyes distant. 'You get to thinking those are voices calling to you. It's something on the wind; a ghost or an Indian chant or something else. You watch the skyline for changes in the sky that mean rain or snow or another drifter's camp. Something in the sky tells a story, and we read the sign just like we do on the trail. And the years slip by. I got so I forgot my age. The last time I thought about it I was thirty-nine. That was some years back. I thought the same might have happened to you. Anyway, I settled here. They got a spot for me out in Boot Hill all paid for including the pine box. I'll settle for that. I had to get off the trail.'

They sipped their beers silently. Cameron wouldn't admit it, but he knew exactly what Monty meant. He had been thinking the same thing himself for some time.

'Well, this is a hell of a nice town,' Cameron said. 'I guess I have been chasing the skyline for some time.'

'What happened between you and Bill Drucker?'

'That was nothing. I had just ridden into town when he threw this boy through a door. I stopped to see what all the commotion was about and this Drucker fella decided to make a show.'

'You sure have a knack for riding into trouble quick.'

'He wasn't much trouble. You and I have seen his kind before. They're mostly yellow.'

'Don't forget the ones with yellow spines are always backshooters.'

'I do expect to see him again.' Cameron laughed quietly.

'Like you said, this is a nice town, but like most places it has its own shadows. Drucker is one, and a rancher named Jim Gilson. His sons, Dave and Steve, are mean hombres. Drucker and them make a fine group when it comes to drinking and gambling. You best stay clear of them. How long are you planning on staying?'

'I haven't decided yet. Does this Gilson own the town?'

'Not a bit, but he has a hankerin' to try. Keep in mind some residents here had family members that died all those years ago in Lawrence when Bloody Bill Anderson rode into Kansas with Quantrill. Folks here haven't forgotten. They stand up for them-selves.'

'Hell, I heard Kansas is almost tame now that Wyatt Earp, Bat Masterson and Luke Short worked with that police commission over in Dodge City.'

'Not quite tame yet, but calming down a bit.' Monty chuckled. 'I heard Wade Hatton retired from being a lawman and Buffalo Bill has his own rodeo show. Times have changed. But not so much that it's all free and easy. There's train robbers in these parts, and a general spooked feeling.'

Cameron glanced over at Sheriff Kerrigan, who was wiping down the bar with a towel. 'What about him? He's not even wearing a gun.'

'He carries a two-shot derringer in his vest pocket. Mostly he has that sawed-off 12 gauge under the bar. He may look like a dandy but he'll fight if he's forced.'

'Good to know.' Cameron took a swallow of beer. 'Any outfits hiring? I could use some pocket money.'

'The widow Drake has a small spread south of town called the Skyline Ranch. That is unless you'd like to sign up with Gilson. He's always taking in strays.'

'I'll pass on Gilson since Drucker rides with him. I've learned to avoid stirring up a hornet's nest when I see one. How many head of cattle does this widow have?'

Monty laughed loudly. 'You might have already stirred up that hornet's nest. But be careful with the widow. She has a few beeves out past the Cottonwood River, and nobody to help except her son. Oh, and she's a real corker, and fast with a Winchester. I can already imagine the trouble you're gonna cause!'

TWO

Cameron thought the stableman, Amos Longstreet, had a face that had more crevices than old leather. The history of the man's life was etched in wrinkles on his tan face, his brown eyes scrutinizing Cameron with distrust.

'Three dollars a week. No exception.'

'You plannin' on getting rich, are you?'

'You pay me up front and if somebody shoots you I can sell your horse and saddle.'

Cameron paid the man in silver. 'Make sure she gets a good rub-down and plenty of oats.'

'I'll look her shoes over, too, at no extra charge, but if she needs iron on her hoofs you have to pay the blacksmith. You plan on staying long?'

'I haven't decided yet. I guess it depends on the poker games.'

'You'll lose it quicker than you make it. I heard you met Bill Drucker.'

'Word travels fast.'

'We don't take much interest in strangers other than making sure they go away or get buried properly.'

Cameron had removed his horse's saddle and draped it over a post in the barn. 'That is real comforting to know.' He took a pitchfork and shoveled some hay into the stall with his horse. 'The rates in this town are high. Maybe I'll find a job.'

'There's jobs west of here in Topeka and maybe way over in Wichita. If you know bulls and heifers you can try Cheyenne. Go south all the way and try Dallas.'

'You sure are friendly. I'm mighty glad I met you today, sort of makes me feel at home.'

That one made Amos smile. Cameron laughed.

'Well since I'm givin' out friendly advice, you should know that all the pretty women in this town are spoken for, except the widow Drake, and she's not friendly at all.'

'I'm not lookin' to get hitched, just to find work.'

'That's what I said thirty years ago. Now I still have a wife up at the house who snores louder than a sick mule.'

Cameron chuckled, brushed his fingers off his hat brim as a salute to the old-timer, and went out. He spent some time in the dry goods store and finally bought a new plaid shirt. His dungarees and boots were still in livable shape, as was his pale Stetson. He bought one box of cartridges although he didn't much like the price. Willow Branch Creek would take all of his money if he wasn't careful.

The main competition for the Big Elk Saloon was the Lucky Ace Saloon, owned by Jim Gilson. The Lucky Ace had been open just a year and at eight o'clock on Friday and Saturday evenings a chorus of girls sang and danced with ostrich fans and not much else. There was a Faro table operated by Ned Patterson who was quite pleased to tell Cameron the sheriff had warned them off Cameron up front.

'The sheriff says you got into it with Bill Drucker. I'm not to serve you any liquor or allow you to gamble here. In fact, Drucker and the boys will be here in town again next Friday. That gives you five days to clear the territory.'

'Is that so?'

'Yes sir. And I work for Jim Gilson, too, and so does Drucker. They already have a spot picked out for you on Boot Hill.'

'Is it shady?'

'What?' Patterson was startled, his eyes wide. Cameron was amused by the man's baffled expression.

'I asked if it was shady. You know, like does my spot have trees over it. When I stretch out I like to be comfortable and dream about senoritas.' Cameron winked at him.

'Why you damn fool! I might enjoy watching them bury you!'

'Yeah,' Cameron drawled, 'that seems to be the

general feeling.'

They had the town locked away from him, all over this one incident with Drucker. He would enjoy settling it, then, although he knew that meant gunplay. He had also quickly defined the conflict between Gilson and the townspeople. Gilson would empty their pockets, and the dancing girls and poker games would appeal to the bachelors as well as the henpecked husbands. The decent folks in Willow Branch Creek would take a grim view of such goings-on. He expected Sheriff Charlie Kerrigan had his hands full.

Cameron spent a day pretending idleness while watching the town. Sheriff Kerrigan spent his mornings in the sheriff's office. His primary duties were to collect taxes, roust the drunks and prevent bank robberies should any such likelihood develop. Cameron doubted the job paid much; probably why Kerrigan supplemented his income as a bartender at the Big Elk Saloon, a far more sedate and respectable establishment than Gilson's Lucky Ace.

He figured at least half of the citizens of Willow Branch Creek were upwards of fifty years old, with the women outliving the men. The profusion of widows created an immediate Sunday congregation for the staid preacher. Cameron noted a few old-timers who had fought at Shiloh or Gettysburg; and as Monty had warned, several residents that had migrated from Lawrence after surviving Quantrill's raid. Those were the people that had the strongest glare of suspicion in their eyes, but he accepted they had earned the right to be suspicious a long time ago.

When his three paid nights at the Timber Ridge Hotel slipped past, he paid for additional time. He was about halfway through Wednesday when he decided that this was, after all, the correct location and his coming here was justified, and his arrival was certainly no accident. It was an unfriendly place, however. His old saddle pal, Monty, was busy at his carpentry, and none of the other townspeople were willing to so much as say howdy. Cameron had his mind set on finding out certain specific details, and when the time was right he'd have a talk with the unfriendly sheriff.

A good hour sitting on a wooden chair on the boardwalk outside the Big Elk Saloon and musing on his uncertain future had settled it. That was when a horse and buggy clattered into view, the woman on the buckboard snapping the reins with determination. She pulled up to the dry goods store and pulled back the wheel brake.

They made eye contact.

She had a golden mane of hair that was tied back with a pink ribbon. She wore a simple blue and white cotton dress that was at odds with her rawhide boots and gunbelt. Her figure was lean and supple. A Winchester rifle was propped on the buckboard with her. Her features, Cameron decided instantly, were as beautiful as any painting or illustration. He had never seen a woman so beautiful and who commanded his attention the way she did. The boy, Randy, sat next to her. He averted his eyes when Cameron looked at him.

Of course, he guessed that she was the renowned widow Drake. She watched him less with curiosity, he thought, than with caution. She climbed off the buckboard with her son and finally looked away. He remained seated, perhaps unwilling to admit that his pulse was pounding. He had half a mind to wave and smile at her, but she looked away and they strode briskly into the store.

Cameron fidgeted, then fidgeted some more. She was undoubtedly confronting Gustav, the shop-keeper, about dismissing her son. Cameron owed the woman an explanation, and he reckoned she would appreciate hearing from him since he had tried to help her boy.

The first thing he noticed when he pushed into the store was the guitar sitting braced up against a stack of flour bags. The guitar was out of place in a store crammed with burlap sacks of wheat and flour, rows of canned goods, new shirts all folded and stacked next to rows of dungarees; and there were axes and pitchforks and shovels. Gustav was handing Randy his wages.

'It ain't my fault, ma'am. He was talking back to Bill Drucker. I can't have a hired hand making folks angry.'

'The kid has a right to stand up for himself,'

Cameron said as he stepped forward.

They all looked at him, and as he passed the guitar he instinctively reached out and pulled it into his hands. 'I'm Cameron Scott, ma'am, and you must be Mrs. Drake.'

'That's right. I'm Becky Drake. Randy told me about you.'

'He was thrown hard and I just helped him up.'

'The best thing that you can do is ride on. Those men will be after you now.'

She held her gaze on him and he sensed neither approval nor disapproval. But her eyes had him; and the way the afternoon light snuck into the doorway and tangled itself in her hair had him, too. He smiled, his fingers gently brushing against the guitar strings.

'That's what people have been telling me since I rode into town. I can't recall ever meeting friendlier folks.' He gave a laugh, and for a moment he thought she might laugh with him, but she remained stoic, her eyes almost hard. He sensed a sadness in her, and that somehow made her all the more appealing.

'I appreciate your standing up for Randy, but none of this needed to happen. We needed those wages.'

'I'll tell you what,' Cameron said looking at Gustav, 'you hire this boy back and give him another chance, and I'll talk to Sheriff Kerrigan and ask him to keep an eye on things so there's no more trouble.'

'Mister, those men are going to beat you to death. The sheriff can't stand up to all of them.' Gustav was red in the face.

'Give me credit for being resourceful. It seems I've been threatened since I came to town.' His fingers strummed the guitar strings. 'I do believe we all need to relax just a bit. Here's an old song my pappy taught me.' He gave Becky Drake as sincere a smile as he could manage, and she looked perplexed, but she also didn't flinch. His fingers found the right chords and it felt good again, just as it had when he learned the song all those years back.

Yippi Ty Yo and Yippi Ty Yay,
I'm riding lonesome and far away.
I wander along through the cool dawn,
That skyline trail that I follow along.
Yippi Ty Yo and Yippi Ty Yay,
I'll ride this trail until the break of day.

He sang in a pleasant baritone that was tinged by the dust of a trail; weathered by the wind and sun, yet still warm and full of heart.

I ride the skyline where the sky is blue,
Where the tall grass whispers under the sun,
Far from home and lonesome for you,
With my pony for company and this old gun.

I'm a skyline rider at twilight,
Lost under the prairie sky,
With an old saddle as my pillow,
I hear your voice among wavering willows,
Calling an end to my plight.

He watched her eyes and saw a gleam, and for a moment Cameron thought she might even tap her foot. Her son, Randy, was visibly interested, his eyes watching Cameron's fingers as they stroked a C chord back and forth.

Yippi Ty Yo and Yippi Ty Yay,
I'm riding lonesome and far away.
I wander along through the cool dawn,
That skyline trail that I follow along.
Yippi Ty Yo and Yippi Ty Yay,
I'll ride this trail until the break of day.

When he finished he gave a short bow and laughed, and then they clapped for him. He set the guitar down and said, 'I might have to buy that thing. Seems I'm out of practice.' Even Gustav was grinning.

'Twenty-five dollars,' Gustav said. 'You can sing, that's true, yes sir!'

'I'd like to learn that,' Randy said quickly. 'I bet I could be taught how to play a guitar.'

Becky glanced at her son, and Cameron said, 'I'll

be glad to teach you what I know.' He looked at Becky. 'I could earn my keep at your place by teaching Randy here some songs and helping around your ranch.'

He said the words as earnestly as possible, but Becky's brow darkened and she blinked rapidly, looking away.

'That's real kind of you, and I could use the help, but. . . .'

'But I'm going to get killed on Friday, and that pretty much does it. Well, shucks, this is the dandiest town. You folks will have me sleeping under the lilies one way or the other.' Then Cameron gave a long, loud laugh, and his laughter boomed in the rafters. Becky watched him carefully, amazed that this brash and likeable cowboy could be so carefree about the danger he faced. She wondered then if he even realized what kind of trouble he was in.

'You don't understand, those men . . .' She hesitated as she looked at him, and stepped toward him. A curl of hair dropped across her face, and as she brushed it away she noticed the look in his eyes and nearly blushed. 'Those men are tough, and I, well, I'd hate to see a nice man like you get hurt.'

'I'll tell you what,' Cameron said. 'If I can work it out that there's no more trouble between me and this Drucker fella then I'll stop by and give Randy a guitar lesson. How's that sound?' He grinned as he said it.

Now she did blush, but she also never broke eye

32

contact with Cameron. 'All right,' she said, 'you keep yourself alive and I'll put you to work. Wages are food and a bunk and guitar lessons for Randy. By the way, my place is called Skyline Ranch. Your song reminded me of it.'

'That's a fine name for a ranch and I appreciate the offer, ma'am, I really do.' He tipped his hat and she turned on her heels and walked out. Cameron resisted the urge to whistle.

'You got trouble! Oh boy, have you got trouble!' Gustav was still grinning.

Cameron shrugged. 'I guess it's a habit of mine.' He gave the shopkeeper twenty-five dollars in silver. 'I better practise on this guitar if I'm going to serenade that pretty lady and teach her son how to play, too.'

Gustav was chuckling and shaking his head in disbelief when Cameron left.

Later that afternoon, after listening to three complaints from the desk clerk about his guitar playing, Cameron heard a train whistle in the distance. Then, outside the hotel, he watched the women and their parasols coming up the street as if flaunting themselves in a parade. They were accompanied by short but handsome men sporting bowler hats and dark wool suits. They looked like people with money, and Cameron could see that they cultivated this impression in their haughty manner and dismissive arrogance. They came right up the street toward him, passed him with but a cursory glance, and checked into the hotel. Three men and three women. The men carried the suitcases and put on a show trying not to look winded. They went to their rooms talking excitedly about the good time they would have at the Lucky Ace Saloon. Their voices clattered up the stairwell like hail striking a tin roof, impossibly loud and irritating.

Cameron noted the women were pretty things, plump and curvy in the right places, and just young enough to be appealing. The Timber Ridge Hotel clerk with the slicked-down hair, Jeffrey, said they were from St Louis.

'St Louis businessmen come all this way to gamble at the Lucky Ace?'

'That's right. Like I told you before, they come from as far away as Chicago.' Jeffrey smirked. 'They leave their wives at home. Mr. Gilson makes sure the ladies they bring are comfortable, too.' He winked knowingly at Cameron. 'You better not play that guitar any more or I'll have to ask you to leave.'

'Sure.'

Cameron went out and walked to the train depot and looked over the engine. The twenty-ton eight-wheel, four-axle steam-powered locomotive sat on the tracks like a giant beast exhaling steam. The cowcatcher rail in the front gleamed in the after-noon light. The coal car was full, set immediately behind the engine, and the two passenger coaches were empty now, but past the windows he could glimpse the plush couches, colored pillows and mahogany bar that made traveling both appealing and comfortable for the businessmen who could afford the steep ticket price. The west had changed, and Cameron wasn't certain if those changes were good or bad.

He approached the conductor, who had emerged from the station office, where the train schedule was tacked up on the wall.

'If you want a newspaper I left them inside. I leave them on the benches after I clean the coach. Some of them are only five days old.'

'No thanks,' Cameron said, 'I was just moseying about.'

'You can mosey about all you want, but you have to pay if you want a ride to San Francisco.'

'I heard there's been train robberies in these parts.'

The conductor squinted suspiciously at Cameron. 'Six months ago, about fifteen miles from here. And one the year before. Are you a lawman?'

'No, like I said, just moseying about.'

'Nosy is more like it. And you look like a lawman.'

'Aw shucks,' Cameron said, trying to sound affable, 'I don't mean to sound nosy. I'm just naturally curious about things. It must be because of all that book learning I've had.'

'Well, be careful. We've got stories about masked riders out along the tracks at midnight. Some say they're ghosts of outlaws or some such craziness.'

Cameron frowned and left the conductor alone.

He thought to himself, *this must be the place after all.* By now the afternoon was waning and a sense of both urgency and loneliness assailed him. Lost in thought, he smoked a thin stick of tobacco and stood watching the main street of Willow Branch Creek when he realized with a start that the Lucky Ace Saloon was the tallest building in town. From his vantage point on the train depot platform he could see that the Lucky Ace was three stories high. It was also the only building without a false front, the peaked roof covered in Spanish clay tiles, a feature that was rare this far north. He had seen beautiful stucco homes with clay-tiled roofs down in Santa Fe and Tucson, but the Spanish influence seemed out of place in Kansas.

Money. It was all about the money. The Lucky Ace Saloon stood like a beckoning angel on the dusty Kansas plain, a jeweled palace just hours by train, connected to St Louis by the steel tracks of the Kansas Pacific Railroad. Catering to the wealthy, and men of influence, Cameron recognized it as a money-grabbing scheme that brought these arrogant men and their women on a 'western adventure'. Tossing his cigarette into the dust, he crushed the sparking quirly with his heel.

The kindest thing he could say at that point was simply that Gilson had a nice set-up. He hadn't even met the man yet but already he disliked him.

With that much money being thrown about it was a sure thing that Gilson's men were loyal. And loyalty bought and paid for could be lethal. He would have to remember that when he faced Bill Drucker on Friday.

THREE

A storm crept in that pounced unexpectedly and lashed the prairie with twisters and rain. The dark wind bent over trees and rattled homes, even knocking over a barn, but otherwise Willow Branch Creek was unscathed, save for muddy streets and a persistent rain that fell from a mountain of purple clouds lingering over the town like a specter.

Cameron stayed in his hotel room reading from the Bible left in the bureau drawer. Occasionally he would stand at the window and watch the people coming and going from the Lucky Ace Saloon. The train had brought a lively group who always seemed happy. There was no sign yet that their luck had run out. Cameron had a strong feeling that would change soon.

Although he was not religious, Cameron enjoyed reading the Bible because reading engaged his mind. His favorite authors were James Fenimore Cooper and Washington Irving. He was familiar with the

Bible, having been fortunate that his mother had insisted that her boy learn how to read. He let his eyes wander over the pages and paused at Psalms 4:27. 'Turn not to the right hand nor to the left: remove thy foot from evil.' Setting the book aside he drifted off and dreamed he was walking on a forest path. A beautiful angel walked at his side, her wings golden and infused with a bright light. When he glanced back their footprints were embedded in the mossy earth, but there was steam rising from the grass and the angel's footprints were cloven. He awoke with a start just as something in his dream too terrible to imagine rushed at him with gleaming fangs.

Rubbing his jaw, he pulled himself off the bed and once again looked out the window. That ominous dark sky had shattered the tranquility, forcing itself onto the town like a belligerent drunk, ugly and unwanted.

He had thought about the direction he might take in solving his problem but he didn't like his options. He would have to choose the lesser of two evils. He didn't want to kill Drucker, yet the man would probably draw on him.

Late that afternoon, he found Monty Gallant at the blacksmith shop forging a horseshoe on a hot fire.

'Expected you to stop in.' Monty said as he slammed the hammer onto the steaming metal. 'You're getting a reputation for asking questions.'

'I'm naturally curious.'

'Are you gonna face Drucker tomorrow?'

'Thought I might speak with him if he holds a grudge. I don't see any reason for us to fight.'

'He might have a different view. When those boys get a belly full of whiskey they tend to cause a ruckus.'

'Do you think Drucker and some of Gilson's men are behind those train robberies?'

'So that's it.' Monty set the hammer down, lifted the horseshoe with metal pliers and dipped it into a bucket of water. 'You have something on your mind that won't quit. Mighty peculiar.'

Cameron laughed. 'I've only been here a few days and anyone can see the timing on Gilson setting up shop and those robberies. I'd say that's peculiar.'

Monty looked hard at Cameron. 'What's your interest in all of that?'

'I like to know what I'm getting into. Seems like a nice enough town even if folks hereabout are a bit ornery.'

'The robberies all happened after some business-men won big at the Lucky Ace. After the second robbery our deputy was killed. They found him about ten miles east. He was shot in the back.'

'That explains why folks are suspicious.'

'That's only part of it. The deputy was Jason Drake, a nice young man. You've already met his son and widow.'

Cameron had to digest the information for a

moment. 'That's why everyone is telling me to be careful. You lost one of your own. Gilson and his men have this town spooked.'

Now it was Monty's turn to chuckle. 'But he doesn't own the town and that does seem to be a sore spot with him. You'll find some friends here, Cam, and when you least expect it you'll have some help. Now don't start snortin' like a bull either. You could end up dead quicker than lightning through a goose.'

'I'm getting an idea on how I might avoid that and work it out with Drucker. We'll see what happens.'

'You always did have ambition, I'll give you that.'

'Can I buy you a beer on Friday?'

'At the Lucky Ace? I wouldn't miss it for anything.'

Cameron left Monty working on forging a new horseshoe.

On Friday morning the sun slanted through a wall of lavender clouds like a bashful bride, but alive with promise. It was enough to lift his mood as he prepared for his day.

Gilson's men rode into town just before noon. Cameron watched them from his hotel window. Drucker rode in front and four men rode behind him. At a glance the five men were no more than average cowpunchers, ranch hands on their day off and coming to town for a drink. One of the men behind Drucker caught Cameron's attention; a fat man with a red walrus mustache. He wore a battered black Stetson that shaded eyes as dark as a reptile's.

Bad men ride together, Cameron thought, *and nothing good will come of this.* But he also knew that he had set his mind to something and he had to play it out.

They wasted no time tethering their horses to the hitching post outside the saloon. It wouldn't take them long now. They would start with the whiskey and chase it with beer.

Cameron pulled his money from his saddle-bag and counted out a hundred dollars in silver. He had an extra fifty in two gold pieces. Stuffing the money in his pocket he went out without his guns. In his previous and quite brief foray into the Lucky Ace he had been told by Ned Patterson, the Faro dealer, that Gilson honored the sheriff's policy of 'no guns in the saloon'. The three barmen all had access to shotguns behind the bar, and Gilson reportedly always had a few armed men upstairs and out of sight. The last thing they wanted was trouble; after all, the Lucky Ace Saloon was profitable. Cameron had a plan and he would stick to it. Hell, he thought, it might even work.

The Lucky Ace Saloon was all walnut, brass and oil paintings of nude women. The stage, built in the rear and no more than ten feet deep, barely held the chorus of dancing girls that sang on weekends, their tightly laced high-heeled boots scuffing the varnished boards. Oil lamps in profusion illuminated the saloon. The paintings themselves were scandalous and boasted titles engraved in brass and fixed

42

onto the ornate frames: *Georgina and the Satyrs, Rosalinda Emerging from a Bath, Susanna Beneath a Pale Moon*, and others of this ilk all went far to encourage bawdy personal reminiscences while imbibing. Expensive cigars were displayed in wooden boxes with red velvet lining. Dogs were not allowed in the Lucky Ace and according to the Faro dealer, Ned Patterson, any women looking like a dog to enter through the scarred batwings would be shot. The whiskey brands were as notorious as the St. Louis bankers that so eagerly filled their glasses with it – Red Tomahawk Whiskey being the best-selling bottle, followed by Mormon Whiskey and Yellow Flower of the Forest Bitters. There was only one brand of beer, Gilson's Beer, which happened to arrive by the barrel, and whose true brewing origin remained unknown, dependent on availability and price. Whiskey drinkers were offered free Arbuckle's coffee on Friday and Saturday nights.

Cameron's initial visit to the Lucky Ace had not prepared him for the full impact of a rowdy Friday-night crowd and the garish opulence of an establishment that catered to the wealthy, but happily fleeced the average working man or cow-puncher.

Monty was sitting at the long polished bar, his boots resting on a brass rail, a wad of tobacco stuffed in his mouth. He chewed, spat into a brass spittoon, and sipped his beer from a tall glass schooner. He smiled at Cameron through tobacco-stained teeth.

'Thought you might show up about this time!'

Cameron idled up next to Monty and said in a low voice, 'Hey listen, go along with what I say. I expect those boys will be ambling over here right quick.'

Monty nodded. 'Pull up a stool and have a beer with me.'

Cameron glanced in the mirror behind the bar hoping to spot Drucker, but the Lucky Ace was a sea of cowpunchers, businessmen and pretty girls serving up drinks. After fifteen minutes Monty said, 'They're set up playing poker in the back room. They'll see you next time one of them wanders to the outhouse. They have to pass us to use the side door.'

'Good. I reckon I'll save them the trouble of looking for me later.'

Monty gave a low laugh. 'Well, you won't have to wait long.'

A few minutes later Drucker was next to him, the whiskey blowing off his breath, his eyes like hot grease bubbling in a pan.

'Somethin' smells in here.'

Cameron eased around on his stool and flashed a calculated smile. 'Aw, let's not start anything again,' he said as good-naturedly as possible, 'I don't want any trouble. Let me buy you a drink, maybe play some poker.'

Still smiling, Cameron opened his palm and showed Drucker the silver coins, and the one gold coin he'd pulled from his pocket. The sight of the glimmering coins had the desired effect. Drucker's eyes widened.

'You wanna play poker?'

'Sure he does,' Monty said, 'but he's not as good as he was before the accident.'

'That's right. I always liked a good game.' Cameron glanced at Monty.

'Accident? What accident did you have?'

Monty, spinning around with his beer glass sloshing foam over his knuckles, said quickly, 'After he got kicked in the head by that mule down in El Paso he should have retired.'

Cameron arched a bemused eyebrow and went along with Monty. 'That's right, Monty was there when I got kicked. Rattled my brains right good.'

'He went off for about five days.' Monty said. 'When he came back to camp he said he got married to a mermaid. No sir, I wouldn't gamble if I was you, Cam, Bill here plays poker with a spirited crowd. You'll lose that money.'

'Now listen here,' Drucker said quickly, 'if this pig stinkin' sheep-herder wants to play poker, I say we let him!'

'That ain't nice,' Cameron said, 'but I don't blame you for being sore at me.'

'We'll be glad to take your money. A dumb hog-farmer don't deserve to spend that money any other way.'

'I might win.' Cameron said.

'You might really be married to a mermaid, too.' Monty said. 'One with a long tail and gills.'

45

Cameron slid from his stool and followed Drucker into the backroom. 'I got a hundred dollars here that says I can win, and since Bill here is angry with me, well, I reckon it's only fair to let him try to win some of this silver. Besides, I'd rather lose at an honest game of poker than have you boys bury me in Boot Hill like I hear you've got planned.'

'Is that what you heard?' Drucker said sarcastically.

'That's right, but why bother? I've got money to lose and more coming in the form of a bank draft from my uncle.'

'Is your uncle wealthy or something?' one man asked.

Cameron nodded. 'But I earned it working on his ranch and I had him save it for me. I reckon this is a good time to have him send it so I sent a telegraph to him.'

'Hell, you're not a bad sort.' Drucker said unconvincingly, 'We've got some whiskey here that'll turn a dog's tail pink. Pull up a chair.'

They set to the task of playing cards. Beer and whiskey were at Cameron's elbow. The fat man with the red walrus mustache was Blake Bullock, foreman for Gilson, and probably the meanest of the bunch. In fact, Cameron had Bullock marked as the strongest threat; he would need to be very careful. The six of them were intent on their cards. The other men were Bob, Deke, Wally and Ray; those four were the least threatening. Drucker and Bullock were it.

Cameron intentionally gave up good cards. His

first hand was three of a kind and he discarded two. His second hand was four of a kind so he gave up three. Slightly disgruntled at having two good hands at the onset, Cameron consoled himself with the knowledge that these men were almost certainly cheating.

After discarding an Ace and a Queen he was content to let these men cheat him out of his money. His intention from the start had been to create the illusion that he was an easy mark in future card games, thus guaranteeing they could make money off him. That would lessen the tension between them while providing Cameron time to accomplish his goals.

Cameron was studying his cards – two of Spades, Jack of Diamonds, three of Clubs, King of Hearts and six of Clubs – when a shadow fell across the table. He looked up directly into the malicious gaze of a man with a horrid scar on his upper lip. His face was shadowed by a salt-and-pepper beard and his brow was obscured by a black Stetson that had seen a lot of wear. The man was tall, dusty from the trail, but powerful-looking. A solitary Colt was holstered on his right hip. Cameron was familiar with the jagged scar on the man's lip because he had given it to him.

Holding his cards in his left hand, Cameron let his right hand slip off the table toward his own holstered Colt. The man saw the movement and broke eye contact with a broad smile as he said, 'Well, this looks like a good game. I sure wish I had time to partake.'

Bullock, looking up, said, 'Where are you from, stranger?'

'St. Louis and then Laramie. I'm heading west on the way to visit my sister.'

'Is that right?' Drucker said, 'Well, we play cards every Friday. You're welcome to try your luck tonight or next week if'n you're still here. There's some businessmen coming on the train from St. Louis that like to play poker.'

'I appreciate that. I might stick around a few days and rest up a bit. Y'all have a good evening.'

Brushing his fingers off his Stetson rim in salute, the man looked at Cameron again and smiled before turning around and exiting the saloon.

An image flashed through Cameron's mind of the man holding his hand to his bloody mouth after Cameron had pistol-whipped him to his knees. Forcing himself to study his cards again, he soon learned that losing at poker didn't require much effort at all now that his concentration had been shattered by a harbinger from his past.

He won a hand, almost out of habit, and Drucker grumbled in discontent. Winning the hand had been an accident. Cameron's concentration was limited as he thought about the man that had grinned at him with a scarred smile.

Larry Strickland, a gambler and worse.

Strickland thought he was tough but Cameron had been tougher. Strickland being in town added to his growing list of concerns, and Cameron wasn't fond of such lethal distractions.

'You gonna need any cards?'

Drucker was staring at Cameron, a thin cigar bent between his greasy lips, his eyes watery from booze.

'Sure, I'll take two. Maybe my luck will change.'

Drucker grunted, slipped the cards across the table. Cameron studied his hand. Two Aces, two sevens and a Jack.

'That slick card shark had his eye on you,' Drucker said.

'Is that right?'

'He figures you for an easy mark. I've seen card sharks before.'

'Hell, if my luck doesn't change I won't have any money for ten days when my uncle's bank draft gets here.'

'Well, if you lose tonight this here is an honest game, so don't go worrying about that card shark.'

'You got it,' Cameron said, forcing a smile.

Bullock, who had been unusually quiet to this point, finally said, 'Just keep losing, pig-farmer. We'll all enjoy spending your money.'

Cameron looked Bullock in the eye. 'I'll bet you will.'

An hour later and Cameron had lost his money as planned. The other players were just a tad too elated, Cameron thought, but other than Larry Strickland's appearance, the night had gone as planned.

After shaking their hands, Cameron made for the

batwing door. He managed to avoid having his silhouette visible in front of the window by slipping outside to his left. There was no movement on the street, but there were also plenty of dark places where a gunman might hide. He breathed a sigh of relief when he arrived at his hotel a few minutes later.

Strickland would have to be dealt with, and so would Drucker and Bullock, but in the meantime Cameron had to fulfill his obligation as an undercover agent for the Pinkerton Detective Agency.

FOUR

They came for him just before sunrise. Cameron was restless and understood the danger he was in. This, coupled with his experience, set him on edge. For this reason he slept lightly and at four o'clock he was wide awake, dressed, and sitting on the side of the bed with his Colt in hand.

His second-floor room at the Timber Ridge Hotel looked out onto the street. There was no balcony, but his corner room was easily visible from an intersection swathed in nighttime shadows. His window was open but the curtains were pulled closed. They were thin curtains made of a cheap fabric that he could see through even in the gloom. Cameron heard what might have been the jingle of a spur down in the darkness.

Something that might have been a voice curled into the dark breeze and lifted itself above the normal sounds of a town still sleeping. He heard it

51

without understanding what was said. The words themselves didn't matter.

Someone was out there.

Cameron stood and drifted to the window but kept to the right. Down in the street he glimpsed a Stetson in silhouette. A door hinge creaked. Shifting his focus, Cameron concentrated on the stairwell outside his room. He believed that someone had just entered the hotel lobby.

Nothing happened for several long minutes; and then for several more long minutes he listened to himself breathe.

At some point his instincts told him that someone was outside of his door. The door was locked but that didn't mean anything.

If they're smart, he thought, *they'll have a man in the street with a Winchester pointed at my window to prevent any potential escape.* One man, maybe two, would break in the door and start shooting. They would expect him to be sleeping but smart enough to know there was a chance he wasn't sleeping at all. Only the more skilled ambusher would factor in that he was actually waiting for them. Cameron was skilled with a six-shooter and wasn't concerned, but neither was he overconfident.

The door slammed into the wall when it was kicked in and the first man stood framed in the doorway with his Winchester blazing. Cameron had moved to right of the door and crouched low with one knee resting on the floor, his right arm extended with the Colt, his left palm cradling the gun to keep the .45 steady as he thumbed the trigger and fired.

The sound of the man's Winchester in the small room was deafening. Cameron's mind registered the flames spurting from the barrel and the harmless thunk of hot lead slapping into his empty bed. Three times the man fired. Cameron's first shot coincided with the man's third shot and shattered his chest, the lead blowing out of his back. He crumpled like a broken rag doll as Cameron fired again, this time at the figure slouched in the hallway.

The man yelped in pain and cursed and Cameron recognized his voice. It was Blake Bullock, the foreman for the Gilson ranch. Cameron didn't recognize the dead man, but he was undoubtedly one of the hired gunmen from the Gilson spread.

Dodging low through the doorway he found Bullock backing down the stars, a red splash growing on his shirt. His pain-wracked gaze fixed on Cameron and he began to raise his gun. Cameron shot him in the chest three times, thumbing the hammer and firing without hesitation. The thundering Colt sounded like an artillery cannon in the small hallway. Gunsmoke clouded the stairwell. Bullock fell back twitching, his eyes staring at the ceiling.

Cameron reloaded. He punched out the hot brass with the ejector and pushed fresh cartridges from his holster into the cylinder. He went down the stairs over Bullock's body without looking at it. No sooner had he reached the landing than Drucker slammed through the hotel doorway with a Winchester. He was staring about wildly. Before he could fire Cameron shot him from his crouched position on the bottom stair.

The bullet did two crucial things. First, it shattered the Winchester's receiver, rendering it useless. Second, the shattered lead ricocheted and cut into Drucker's belly. He dropped the rifle and clutched his bloody belly, stumbling backward out the hotel door, his wails of agony slicing through the morning stillness.

Cameron went after him.

Dashing out onto the boardwalk nearly proved fatal as a slug tore a hole in the wall next to him. Glancing at Drucker he saw the smoke curling from his rifle but by now the pain was too much. Drucker was fading rapidly. He dropped the rifle into the dust and clamped both hands across his belly. He sank to his right knee moaning. Cameron felt a twinge of regret for the man.

'Why did you come after me?' he asked.

Drucker winced and gasped. 'We heard . . . about you . . . heard you was a Pinkerton. . . .'

So Strickland had talked, Cameron thought.

'You should have left me alone,' he said.

'A Pinkerton. . . .' Drucker gasped. 'Now I'm gut-shot.'

'Easy now. I can get a doctor.'

'No, I'm done for . . . Gilson is gonna come now, so you better. . . .'

Drucker's eyes rolled white and he slumped to his left and twitched and died. Cameron holstered his Colt, took his Stetson off and wiped his sweating face with his neckerchief. The street was still empty but he knew that wouldn't last. Early as it was, Willow Branch Creek was about to come and have a look at the commotion, and so too would the sheriff.

There wasn't long to wait. Up the street the shopkeeper Gustav came out and stood on the boardwalk looking over at Cameron. Sheriff Charlie Kerrigan came out of his office looking half asleep, irritated as hell and carrying a shotgun.

'Don't pull your gun,' he said as he approached.

'Hell, Sheriff, I'm not looking for trouble. These men came after me. I had no choice but to defend myself. There's two more inside.'

Sheriff Kerrigan studied on Cameron a bit longer than Cameron liked, but he made no sudden moves. Presently he said, 'All right, let's go inside and you tell me what happened.'

Once inside, the sheriff looked over Bullock. Cameron told him what had occurred, leaving nothing out.

'He came at you through the door?'

'And this one up here. I've never seen that one before.'

The sheriff went up the stairs and nudged the

corpse to look at the face. 'That's Steve Gilson, one of Jim Gilson's sons. You're in a hell of a deep patch of quicksand, pardner.'

'Yeah,' Cameron drawled, 'I'm sure happy that I stopped in this friendly town.'

'I'm putting you in jail for your own damn good.' Kerrigan raised his shotgun. 'You and I are about to see what a mean old son-of-a-bitch like Jim Gilson is going to say when he finds out his youngest son is heading up to Boot Hill.'

Cameron shrugged and raised his hands. 'Like I said, this sure is a friendly town.'

Stripped of his gun, Cameron found himself on a squeaky cot with a bad mattress in the Willow Branch Creek jail. He waited for Sheriff Kerrigan to lock the cell before he spoke up.

'Sheriff, there's something you should know.'

Kerrigan eyes him suspiciously. 'What's that?'

'I'm a detective for the Pinkerton Agency. I've got a letter here that spells it all out. I'm investigating those train robberies you've been having.'

'Let's see the letter.'

Cameron pulled the letter from his vest pocket and gave it to the sheriff. Kerrigan read it quickly, folded it up again, and returned it to Cameron.

'I don't suppose this situation could get any more complicated,' he said.

'Actually,' Cameron said with half a grin, 'it could.'

'How so?'

'There's a man named Larry Strickland in town.

You'll know him by the scar on his face. I put it there.'

'And you think he's here to gun you?'

'It could be a coincidence, but he's not up to anything good. Drucker told me before he died that he'd talked with Strickland. I helped put Strickland in jail a few years back.'

Sheriff Kerrigan's face mapped out his unhappy reaction. Cameron saw the anger flare in his eyes and his features turn red.

'You might have said something when you came to town about being a Pinkerton. That carries a lot of weight. Now you've gone and killed one of the Gilson boys, and two of Gilson's gunmen. I should hang you just on principle. Now I'm going to have a hard time keeping the lid on this town.'

Kerrigan stomped out of the room, much to Cameron's surprise. He'd expected to be released from jail once the sheriff learned that he worked for the Pinkerton Agency. There was nothing to do now but sit on the squeaky cot and wait. Fifteen minutes passed. After thirty minutes Cameron was downright irritated although his features didn't show it. He stretched out on the cot and allowed his body to relax. His breathing was calm, but his mind was in turmoil. Strickland had messed things up fairly quickly. Cameron decided the man's appearance had to be an unfortunate coincidence.

An hour passed before Kerrigan returned. He unlocked the cell and said, 'All right, you're clear.

I've got witnesses that saw those men heading for the hotel with their guns drawn. But I want you to leave town.'

Cameron nearly bounded off the cot, happy to be out of the stuffy cell.

'Look here, Sheriff,' he said, 'I've got a job to do. Leaving town isn't part of my plan. I'm not the type of man that gives up on things.'

'Then find another way to come at it.' The sheriff ran his palm over his unshaven face. Cameron realized it was still quite early in the morning. 'Let me spell this out for you. I have to take Jim Gilson his son's body. That could start a war. I'll have to deputize some men to go with me just to guarantee my own safety. I'd like to tell him that you're a long way on the trail when I do that.'

Cameron thought it over a moment. Then he said, 'Look, deputize me and let me talk with Gilson, and then I'll leave once you're out of it. I'll state my case, and I won't leave out that I'm a Pinkerton man.'

Kerrigan nodded. 'That might work, but you can't stay in town, and you know he's going to come after you eventually.'

'That's going to be my problem, Sheriff.'

'All right. I'll get the men together. Strap your gunbelt back on and stay put.'

It took Kerrigan another hour to get a small group of deputies together and have the bodies stretched out in a buckboard. Cameron was pleased that Monty

Gallant was one of the deputies. The other deputies were Dan Hockman, a rancher with an experienced, hardened look; and Bob Robeson, a tall, rugged gundog from Iowa who had married the local school-marm and worked for the Union Railroad. Cameron thought they were both good choices and they were loyal to the sheriff. Next to his old friend, Monty, he sensed that Robeson would be a good ally in a gun-fight.

After lifting the bodies of Bullock, Drucker and Gilson into the buckboard and covering them with a canvas tarp, the riders set out for the Gilson ranch.

The sheriff handled the buckboard with Monty next to him. Hockman and Robeson rode behind the buckboard and Cameron rode on the right side closest to the sheriff. The Gilson ranch was a solid fifteen miles from town although most of the trip was along a well-worn trail. Cameron studied the coun-tryside hoping to spot a location that might serve as a hiding place. Having once been outnumbered five to one in an ambush he had learned the benefit of adapting to situations on the run. This, of course, was not cowardice on his part but rather a learned sur-vival mechanism.

'Are there any canyons or arroyos beyond this stretch of forest?' he asked the sheriff.

Kerrigan nodded. 'Down near the widow Drake's place. There's rolling hills and several creeks that connect to the Little Bear Creek and Cottonwood River. A few canyons are further west. Are you planning on hiding out?'

Cameron had to laugh. 'Well, you're very percep-tive, Sheriff. Not that leaving your friendly town is something that I'd like to do, but given the circum-stance I'd better hole up somewhere and see how things develop.'

'That strikes me as a potentially unhealthy activity. If I were you I'd ride all the way back to Chicago and stay there.'

This time it was Monty that laughed, and loudly.

'I can tell you one thing, Sheriff, this here rascal has never run from a fight in his life and he's not about to start now!'

When they came close to the Gilson ranch Cameron was impressed by the main house. It was a big log house with a wrap-around porch. The bunkhouse and stables were equally spacious, but set back from the main building. A few drovers watched them sullenly as they entered the gate, and Jim and Dave Gilson came out on the porch to look at them. They saw the buckboard and perhaps some instinct allowed them to guess at its contents.

'Who's been killed?' Jim Gilson demanded.

Cameron spurred his horse up but slightly off to the side. 'Mister Gilson, I had to kill your son along with Drucker and Bullock. They came gunnin' for me. I had no choice.'

They all saw the searing anger flare in Gilson's fea-tures as he came off the porch and walked to the buckboard. Kerrigan and Monty eased themselves off the buckboard and joined Gilson, who had pulled back the tarp. He cursed loudly. Gilson wasn't wearing a gun, but his son Dave wore a holstered Colt. His eyes never left Cameron, and Cameron kept an eye on him.

The sheriff explained what happened and finished by saying, 'I have statements from the witnesses that this was self-defense. I'm sorry about your son, but don't come to town looking for trouble.'

Gilson's eyes bore into Kerrigan. 'You son-of-a-bitch, you better remember something. I own this territory. I made it all mine and no measly barkeep with a tin star can tell me what to do!'

'Now Jim, like it or not I'm the law. I will uphold the law even against you. Don't push your luck with me.'

Cameron was impressed with Kerrigan all the more. Gilson glanced at Hockman and Robeson with disdain, and then came around to glare up at Cameron.

'You're a dead man,' he said. 'I'll find you one day or one of my men will. I hear you work for the Pinkerton's. I'll send them a condolence letter.'

With that Gilson strode away after barking orders for his men to remove the bodies from the buckboard. He and Dave disappeared into the house.

When the bodies were removed Monty let out a long whistle. 'Let's ease out of here, boys.'

Hockman and Robeson rode the backtrail as they turned around. A crow landed on the frame of the antlered gate and cawed eerily at them as they passed beneath it. The crow's shrill cry lingered in the air like an omen.

FIVE

They rode back to town and Cameron fetched his belongings from the hotel. Sheriff Kerrigan waited in the street for him with Hockman and Robeson still astride their horses. Monty stayed back on his horse and watched from a distance. The sheriff had returned to his office after announcing he understood that Cameron was good as his word about leaving.

'What are you doing with a guitar?' Hockman asked as Cameron lashed it to his saddle.

'I like to warble like a bird,' Cameron said merrily. 'You should hear me after a glass of whiskey. I'm a regular thespian!'

Hockman and Robeson glanced at each other curiously.

Robeson said: 'Where do you plan on going?'

Cameron, who had been thinking about the widow Drake's agreement to teach her son some guitar music while doing chores had decided to keep that important fact quiet. He had also decided that he wasn't going to visit the Drake ranch just yet, not with Gilson and his men almost certainly on the hunt for him. 'I'm open to suggestions,' he said, looking up at Robeson.

'I'd stay clear of Gilson. His sons are the trouble but he can't see through them. He's all twisted up, like he knows that he's lost control and he hates himself for it.'

'All right.'

Robeson looked up at the sky pensively and then back at Cameron. 'Those boys are mean down to their bones. Old man Gilson wasn't always like that, but he's like that now.'

Hockman, who had been listening quietly, said, 'That's a fact.'

Monty came up on his horse. 'I won't ask what your plan is.'

'That's good,' Cameron said.

'If you tell me what the plan is I wouldn't be surprised anyway.'

'No, you wouldn't.'

'But I know you have a plan because that's the way you are.'

'I suppose.'

'So what's the plan?'

Cameron, feigning surprise, said, 'What plan?' Then he smiled and pulled himself into the saddle. 'Well, boys, I hate to leave this friendly town but it's time I said *adios.*'

Robeson at least was chuckling as a baffled Monty and Hockman watched Cameron spur his horse and ride out.

Cameron rode west and followed the railroad tracks. Although he wasn't about to reveal his plans, even to a friend like Monty, he had already decided on a course of action, at least in general terms. His original task was to uncover the train robbers, which had been easy enough. Still, he had no solid proof but it was obvious that Gilson and his sons were responsible for the robberies, and somehow it tied in with the gamblers that visited Willow Branch Creek from St Louis. It was all too convenient.

His immediate concern was to sidetrack the men he knew would be hunting him. His destination was Prairie Hollow, a town he had passed on his way to Willow Branch Creek. It was dark when he entered the town. Yellow light spilled out of the solitary saloon along with the sounds of an off-key piano, giggling doves, and raucous laughter.

The old man that worked the blacksmith shop and stable was snoring on a smelly bale of hay when Cameron walked his horse into the barn. Cameron looked around. It would do until morning, and the man smelled like whiskey. Identifying Cameron accurately later would be difficult for him. Cameron stabled his horse, set the saddle on the fence, and pitchforked hay into the stall before waking the man up and paying him to keep the horse safe until morning. The old coot grumbled his thanks, pocketed the coins, scratched at a fat tick that was clinging to his eyebrow, and went back to sleep.

The hotel was another matter. The proprietor was also asleep, but this time in the back room. The lanky man looked to be about thirty, and as henpecked as a man could be. His white shirt was stained yellow at the collar, and his wedding ring was embedded in swollen fingers. When Cameron woke him up he said, 'Damn it all to hell! I can't even get a decent night's sleep with my wife off visiting her ailing sister. I might have done better running a dove's parlor than buying this danged hotel!'

The room was clean and Cameron lay on the bed without undressing. He had unbuckled his gunbelt, propped his rifle, guitar and bedroll in the corner, and stretched out with his Colt in his hand and fell asleep immediately. His inner clock would wake him in a few hours. He slept without dreaming; a quick hard sleep that rested his fatigued mind and body.

His objective was to rest, and make his presence known just enough to create some confusion, and then he planned on riding back and hiding out near Willow Branch Creek while he surveyed the area and planned his next move.

He woke before dawn. A rooster was strangling the morning solitude with a throaty anthem as Cameron saddled his horse in the stable. Once he had his gear – rifle, bedroll and guitar – secured he gave the snoring stableman a light kick on his boots and woke him up. After a few prefatory curses from the disgruntled man, Cameron thanked him and pointedly mentioned that he was riding south to Yuma.

By the time he rode back the sun was high and the day tilted toward the deep shadowed solitude and blue-sky afternoons that are so treasured in summer on the frontier. So it was that he sat astride his horse on a hill half a mile from the Drake ranch and watched a pretty woman and her son move back and forth from the barn as they did their morning chores. The two were but specks in the distance but he could make them out well enough to be certain who they were. She had called the place Skyline Ranch. The name fit. The house and barn were built on a prairie that bordered the forest in the east, rolling green hills in the south, and a tangle of woodlands and small hills in the west, all of which was intersected by a bubbling creek that crawled in from the north. She had some cattle, chickens, pigs, and horses. He counted two dozen cows and a few bulls, just enough to make some money and feed themselves.

What bothered him was the absence of ranch hands. There was a small bunkhouse that appeared empty. Becky and Randy were handling all of this by themselves. He felt a pang of guilt because she might still be expecting him and it wasn't time yet. He needed a few days to look into this peculiar problem about train robberies.

Cameron lingered on the hillside watching them just a tad longer than he should have, but finally he tugged the reins and cantered away. He circled the ranch. She had about thirty acres. It was small compared to Gilson's spread, but the widow Drake had the best water supply and a long pasture with tall grass. The forest and hills made a natural barrier, and she was close enough to town to sell beef and eggs easily or buy her own supplies.

Just her and the boy, he thought, *now isn't that something!*

Those deeply wooded hills appealed to him. The pines were tall and thick, and on a summer's day the scent of pine was nearly intoxicating. Cameron loved the rugged, outdoor life. He rode into the hills and nosed around a bit until he found a spot that he liked. The clearing he found was no more than fifteen feet across, but set high on the hill and surrounded by a thick stretch of pines and scrub-brush. There was enough grass for his horse. He could water the horse by sneaking down to that creek near Skyline Ranch. He only planned on staying up here a few days, and his meager food supplies would be enough.

After unsaddling his horse he got to work making a lean-to so the rain didn't soak him. Using a Bowie knife, he cut some long branches free of the scrub and made a frame. Then he cut smaller, leafy branches into sections and secured them over the top. It was crude, but it would keep him dry. He stowed his guitar, bedroll and rifle under the lean-to. After hobbling his horse nearby, he wandered about the hillside to get a feel for the land.

His secret location turned out to be better than he anticipated. He was greeted with a partial view of the railroad tracks half a mile away on the other side of Skyline Ranch. Beyond that was the Gilson land. The thought struck him that Gilson must surely have his eye on the Drake property. Skyline Ranch would add another level of profitability to Gilson's substantial spread.

That first night he hunkered down without a fire. He thought it wise not to take any chances, so although he had a powerful taste for coffee, he settled for water from his canteen. The stars above burst free of the lavender sky and shone like silver. He felt confident, but he also knew that Gilson would be hunting for him. He had seen it in the man's eyes. Without realizing he had done it, his Colt was in his hand, and he had flipped open the loading gate and plunged a sixth cartridge into the chamber he normally left empty with the hammer resting on it for safety. Cameron was determined to be ready for anything Gilson could throw at him.

SIX

Jim Gilson stood over his son's grave with his fists clenched at his sides. They had buried Steve Gilson next to his mother in the small plot behind the ranch house. The other bodies had been taken away and buried in a patch of earth near the field where the cattle grazed amid the tall grass. Jim Gilson instructed his men to fence that plot in and make appropriate crosses for his fallen ranch hands. For the first time in his life he was glad that his wife wasn't alive. The death of Steve would have been too much for her.

Gilson knew that his sons had gone bad. He knew it as a fact that was as certain as the sun rising every morning. They had gone bad like apples sitting on the bottom of a maggot-infested barrel and rotting away. What he didn't understand was how that had happened. He glanced at his son Dave who stood next to him at the grave. Behind them stood Larry Strickland.

Dave was tall, taking after his mother, with wavy brown hair. At one time the girls in town all fancied him, but whatever had eaten away at him had changed all of that. There was something in him that his father couldn't define; something dark that had twisted his soul into a knot. Steve had become like that, too. The evil showed on their features. It clung to their eyes and shadowed their brows. The girls had stopped liking them. The ranch hands barely tolerated them.

When had he lost control over them? Maybe their mother's sudden death from a fever seven years earlier had been part of it. She had been a calming influence on them. Whatever it was, Jim Gilson had been unable to stop it.

He knew without a doubt that Steve had got what was coming to him. That Pinkerton man, Cameron Scott, had only been defending himself. Sheriff Kerrigan wouldn't lie. The problem was that this was his son, and Dave wouldn't let his brother's death go unavenged. Not by a long shot. Cameron Scott would be tracked down and gutted like a deer after the hunt.

What could he do to stop it?

Nothing. Jim Gilson thought long and hard about the changes in his life, and the sacrifices his wife had made to start this family. That had all been a long time ago, but he had never forgotten it. Maybe he didn't want to stop it. Maybe there was too much blood on all of their hands to stop any of this. The

71

best he could hope for would be to keep Dave alive, and by keeping him alive maybe they could find a way back to being the family that his mother had loved.

'Have the boys make a cross,' he said to Strickland. 'Later on I'll have a stone marker brought in for him.'

Watching Strickland go he wondered about this strange man. He had come to them after Steve was killed and told them about Cameron Scott. He was a Pinkerton man probably investigating those train robberies. Dave had brought Strickland into his confidence and explained the set-up. Gilson paid for the train fare for a select group of businessmen to visit Willow Branch Creek and 'play poker in the wild west'. These men were all fancy boys, dudes without any experience, their only redeeming quality in Gilson's eyes being that they all had money. Lots of money. One of the attractions was the 'danger' of being out west, in addition to the soiled doves who plied their trade with an unmatched skill in seduction.

The train robberies had been carefully staged to add a sense of danger and entice them to come back. Gilson made certain that they never lost all of their money, but just enough to add some weight to his own pockets. The dudes were dumb enough to fall for it. That, and the bedroom attractions offered by Gilson's hand-picked doves, had earned Willow Branch Creek and the Lucky Ace Saloon a reputation as a Babylonian oasis out west for sex, gambling and cavorting. It was precisely what those starched shirts in St. Louis needed now and again.

Something about Strickland rubbed Gilson the wrong way. He wished his son hadn't confided in him. Now they really had no choice but to invite him to work for them, but Gilson didn't like it. Something about the man was just wrong.

Years before, Gilson had encountered a charlatan named Doc Crenshaw whose wagon advertised 'A Magic Elixir That Will Cure Your Ills!' Crenshaw had that same demeanor that gave Gilson the sense that he was being taken advantage of. Strickland was like all of those phony snake-oil salesmen that roamed the west, and he hated them.

For some time he had nurtured the idea in secret that he could prevent his sons from continuing their evil ways. He had the power to stop them, but that would mean they might end up dead or in jail. Now that one of his sons was dead, he pondered what might happen to Dave. He was intent on avenging his brother's death, and Gilson knew that only a bullet would stop him. What could he really do now?

Dave was talking about what he would do to the Pinkerton man.

'I'm gonna cut him open and watch him die slowly as he holds his own innards in his hands.'

'Don't forget the law is on his side. He hasn't broken any laws and we'll have to be careful how we approach him.'

'The law doesn't mean anything to me! That sheriff is all talk. Besides, I'll catch that Pinkerton bastard all by his lonesome self. It'll be self-defense, and that's all we have to say. Not even that tin star Kerrigan will go against your word, Pa.'

'I expect not.'

It was late in the day before all of the burials were finished, and Gilson managed to convince both his son and Strickland that they should wait until morning before riding out. Dave didn't like it but conceded they'd have a better chance of picking up Cameron's trail if they left just before first light.

That night Jim Gilson dreamed that his wife was standing in a field among yellow wildflowers with the sun tangled in her hair. She smiled and beckoned to him. Gilson ran toward her but while his legs were pumping furiously she never came any closer. She was always just out of reach, urging him on, the heady scent of pollen and the sound of birds chirping all echoing in the air with a steady rhythm. Then her face changed to terror and she was screaming. He couldn't hear what she said but her lips formed the word 'Run!' Glancing behind he saw a wall of purple clouds dip toward the ground the way waves fold upon themselves before striking a beach. The air around him had turned cold. Then he realized that he was standing just inside the shade, isolated from the sunlit world from where his wife still beckoned to him urgently. He looked down at his feet. He was running but the shade around him was not only growing, it was also turning darker. The scent of pollen and the chirping of birds were replaced by a steady sound of galloping hoofbeats. There in the distance behind him, and gaining on him with each passing second, six dark-cloaked skeletons with flaming eyes grinned malevolently as they whipped their steeds toward him. The horses were black and their eyes too emitted pulsing flames. Gilson screamed, reaching for his wife, but she shrank into the sunlit grass, forever out of his reach.

In the morning his head ached terribly. After having his housekeeper make their breakfast, he instructed his son and Strickland to place extra ammunition in their saddle-bags. Each of them wore a Colt single-action revolver and carried a '73 Winchester in a leather scabbard. Standard weapons for the west, but the amount of extra ammunition was unusual even for the ever-cautious Gilson. This Pinkerton man wasn't going to be given any chance whatsoever.

Prairie Hollow was the closest town, and they all agreed it was the logical place to begin their search. The first person they spoke with was the henpecked hotel proprietor. Gilson was surprised when the man immediately blurted out, 'Yeah, he was here! He woke me the hell up! I was sleeping off a pint of Wild Hog whiskey when he came barging in with that guitar and his bedroll.'

'That's him. What did he say?'

'He only said he was sleeping here a few hours.

The stableman is Reilly and he might know more.'

Reilly, the cranky stableman, was less prone to share information than the gossipy proprietor was. Dave Gilson knocked him hard across the head with his fist and pushed him into a stall where he forced him onto his back and put his knee into his chest while holding his Colt to the man's forehead.

'Yuma!' the man said with his eyes bugging from his head. 'He said he was going to Yuma!'

Yuma didn't make sense to them. Neither Gilson nor his son believed it and Strickland was adamant that the man was lying. Gilson, however, didn't believe the man was lying. He surmised it was more likely that Cameron Scott had led the man to believe he was riding to Yuma to throw them off his trail. The problem was that in order to prove it they would have to ride on, and because of his commitments Gilson wouldn't allow it.

'We're riding back,' he announced, 'and that can work to our advantage. If this Pinkerton man is still in the area we'll find out about it. When he makes his presence known we'll kill him. Until then we say nothing and go about our business.'

The next day they were too tired to do much of anything although Dave proclaimed that he would ride to town and have a bathtub filled with whiskey before having a dove join him in a whiskey bath that would keep them drunk for a month. Being a braggadocio also meant, as all of the ranch hands knew, that Dave would have trouble finishing one bottle of whiskey that very afternoon. In fact, Strickland found him snoring in the barn with the scent of whiskey assailing the small pig that was snorting about his smelly boots. Dave was slumped against a bale of hay with the half-finished bottle still clutched in his hand, his mouth open to let the tonsorial thunder escape from his parched throat.

The other ranch hands reported an absence of news. There was no sign of the Pinkerton man, as they expected, but Jim Gilson held onto the idea that Cameron Scott was hiding out in the area.

Gilson was up and dressed before sunrise the next day. He demanded that his son and Strickland saddle up. He was in a foul mood. Black-cloaked demons with fiery eyes had pursued him in his dreams. His son was bleary-eyed and sluggish; the whiskey had taken him down a notch. The damn fool didn't know when to stop. Strickland was sullen, and Gilson had a mind to cut him loose after they had enacted their plan when the poker game was finished. The visitors from St Louis were arriving and he wanted to keep his plan secure, but afterwards there was no reason to keep Strickland around.

The sound of thundering hoofbeats shattered the morning's tranquility as they rode from the Gilson ranch. Murder boiled like hot grease upon Gilson's fevered mind. Any thought of his wife's kindness was lost in the blood-colored morning sky as they began to hunt for Cameron Scott.

SEVEN

He waited, hidden deep within the seclusion of the tall pines. Some inner instinct had awakened him. This instinct, born of experience, had helped keep Cameron alive through several adventures. It was time they came hunting for him. He sensed it, and he embraced their pursuit without fear. Let them come.

No doubt Gilson would have questioned Strickland for some insight into Cameron's behavior, but Strickland's knowledge was limited. They would learn only that he was dangerous. A Pinkerton man had to be dangerous.

Having gone over the territory carefully, Cameron had left no sign of his presence. Cameron had kept the trails clear of horse apples and hoof prints. Unless they rode directly up to him, which meant riding a haphazard trail through dense underbrush, they should never see any sign of him. Still, Cameron accepted that anything was possible, so he had mentally prepared himself for a quick escape. He was also prepared for the possibility of a gunfight. It was the gunfight he wanted to avoid.

The sun had just cracked the horizon when he saw dust on a far trail. They were riding hard and fast, but still not in his direction. He guessed they would make a wide circle looking for signs of a lone rider. The area where he was hidden was comprised of a series of hills and hillocks that curved like a horse-shoe for ten miles. Finding Cameron might be the equivalent of finding a needle in a haystack, but that was no reason to relax. His rifle was loaded and in his hand as he made his way on foot from his camp.

He found a spot on a hill three miles away. His horse was hobbled in a secluded glen and munching at the tall grass near his camp. He sat back from the cliff-side and looked over a plain of grass. The prairie swept west and beyond that was Becky Drake's ranch. He was overdue to visit her and talk about that job she had offered, and he wondered if she was irritated with him. He thought he might sneak down and pay her a visit soon.

He finally saw the riders but they were small specks in the distance. They still gave no indication of riding in his direction; they appeared to be circling the area looking for hoof prints.

Waiting was always difficult. Although Cameron could be a very patient man, being patient was still difficult when killers roamed the prairie. He wanted to get on with it, but getting on with it meant waiting.

So he waited, conscious of his rifle's weight in his hand.

He thought they might be moving closer to Becky's ranch but he had lost sight of them. They could be anywhere except straight in front of him which, from this vantage point, was an area that spanned five miles in most directions.

He didn't like the idea that they would visit Becky and question her about him, although he accepted that it was inevitable. His instinct told him that Becky would keep quiet about her offering him work. The boy he wasn't sure of, but he doubted if they would question him. Becky was an easy target for a lot of reasons, not least of which being that she was pretty.

He wanted to sneak in close to the ranch and keep an eye on things, but managing to stay out of sight while on foot would be difficult. To reach the ranch he would have to cross about two miles of open prairie before reaching the distant treeline that bordered Becky's ranch. He couldn't chance it.

Looking out over the expanse of tall grass swaying in the summer wind, and further out to the hills and ridges thick with trees, he thought it was a big country in some ways but small in others. He never would have imagined encountering his old friend Monty Gallant in this faraway prairie town, but he had. And then there was Strickland. What were the odds that he would cross-trail with a man that he had helped send to prison for two years?

Larry Strickland was a lot of things, but the main

thing he was good at was being greedy. He was greedy and reeked of it. His greed clung to him like a layer of perspiration and soiled his clothes.

Cameron had been a split second away from killing him when he changed his mind and pistol-whipped him to his knees instead. Now he wondered if killing him hadn't been the better option. Strickland had been stealing horses while working as a deputy sheriff down in Hawk Hollow, a Kentucky border town north of Memphis. He had run up a gambling debt and the horses were a way to pay his debt. The Pinkerton Detective Agency had sent Cameron to investigate at the request of a wealthy horse breeder, and once things had unraveled, Strickland had attempted to escape. That was when Cameron had caught up with him in the barn. Strickland had gone for a derringer in his vest and Cameron had laid him out, leaving a scar on Strickland's face.

The bastard had only drawn two years because of the sympathy he elicited as a result of his public service as a deputy sheriff. Cameron wasn't fooled. The man was as dirty as they get.

The sun was high when he spotted dust on the trail in the distance. The three riders were galloping across the plain and heading for the ridgeline on his right. He studied them as they rode closer. Old man Gilson was in the lead, and his son and Strickland rode side by side behind him.

For the next three hours he watched them

search the hills, but the closest they came to him was half a mile away. The area was too large, the forest too deep. Cameron figured they had searched Becky's place earlier. It was late afternoon when the riders turned and rode off toward the Gilson ranch.

The sun had dipped below the treeline when he saddled his horse. Slipping the Winchester into his scabbard, and slinging his guitar over his shoulder, he spurred his horse and started down the trail.

Becky's ranch wasn't that far, but he was still cautious when he crossed the open plain. Once inside the trees he made his way easily over the hills and into the valley where Skyline Ranch gleamed like an oasis in the twilight. Yellow light spilled from the cabin windows, and there was a lantern in the barn. He could see the lantern hanging on a hook inside the barn door when he cantered through the gate.

Randy came out of the barn holding the lantern.

'Ma said to watch out for you. Gilson and his son were here looking for you. They had another fella with them I haven't seen before.'

Randy held the lantern up to get a better look at Cameron.

Cameron dismounted. 'Hold that lantern away, Randy. I'd hate to be shot before I tasted your ma's cooking.'

Randy grinned. 'Aw, those men are gone. They looked all tired to me. Dave Gilson looked downright sick.'

82

'Is that right? Well, maybe they'll stay off the trail a spell. Why don't you tell your ma I'm here while I get this horse some oats.'

'Plenty of oats in the barn,' Randy said, 'and hay, too.'

Cameron unsaddled his horse and locked it in a stall where the horse went to work munching on hay. He brought the guitar and rifle with him when he went to the house.

Becky was setting an extra place at the table when he walked in. He took off his hat. She was wearing a blue cotton shirt and brown trousers. Her hair was tied back in a bun and there was a smudge of dirt on her face. Her cheeks were flushed red, as if she had exerted herself. She smiled at him when he walked in. Cameron thought she was the most beautiful woman he had ever seen.

'Howdy, Cam. I thought you might stop over. Gilson was here looking for you, but there's nothing to worry about now.' Just like that, and she had made it all seem natural. 'Now sit down and we'll eat.'

Cameron took off his hat and let it hang from the back of his chair. Becky served up a bowl of steaming potatoes, chicken, carrots and some freshly baked bread. She had coffee and milk, too, and Cameron treated himself to the coffee. It was a sight better than the coffee he'd brewed for himself up in the hills.

They made small talk while they ate. Randy was interested in the guitar. He kept eying it while they ate. When they were finished eating Cameron fetched his guitar and tuned it quickly. Then he sat down in the chair.

'I hope we have more time later,' he said, 'and I can show you how to tune this.' Cameron plucked at the strings. 'This is how you make the C chord.' His finger pressed a fret. 'This is the D chord.'

Cameron went back and forth showing Randy the difference between the C and D chord. 'The E chord is a little different. It goes like this.'

Randy watched earnestly as Cameron strummed the guitar. He hummed and then showed him how to pluck the A minor, D and C chords, setting his fingers just right. Randy appeared mesmerized, but after a few minutes he demonstrated a natural ability with the guitar chords.

'It just takes practice. Most of the songs I know use just a few chords. It isn't that difficult once you get the practising done. You have to keep at it.'

Without realizing it at first, Cameron had begun to pick out a song that his pappy had taught him a long time past.

That long river took me away,
Away to the sagebrush and faraway hills;
Down a lazy river with my heart led astray
Where the land offered sacrifice and too many
  ills,
Down that long river to the faraway hills.

Ole San Antonio I wish I were home
Home from these trails I endlessly roam,
Ole San Antonio I wish I were home
And away from the lonesome wind that does
    moan.

Ole San Antonio my bones have grown old,
Ole San Antonio my heart has grown cold,
I've been away so long and need to come home
And all I have left is my horse and a song.

Randy's eyes had brightened and he stomped his
foot to the rhythm. Cameron sang a few more lines
before setting the guitar down.

'That's about it. I'll tell you what, I'll leave this
guitar here while I take care of my business, and
when I return I'll teach you a few songs. Meantime,
you just practise what I taught you as best as you can
remember.'

'That's real nice of you, Mr Scott, I really mean it!'

'Call me Cam or Cameron. I'm glad to help out.'

Becky had made fresh coffee and brought him a
cup. They drank their coffee together without
speaking. When they had finished, Cameron played
another little ditty his pa had taught him, and said
to Randy, 'Here's a short one. I strum it a little
faster.'

Will you take me back my darlin,' and will you
    bring me home?

My days are long and I'm so old and no more
   can I roam.
The prairie is cold and the rivers are wide,
But I'll cross them all to be at your side,
Oh, I'll cross them all to be at your side.

Cameron said while he was here he'd better help out
so he had Randy show him around the place again to
get a feel for the equipment they had. She had a
sturdy shovel and fence wire in the barn, logs stacked
for fence posts, hay for the horses, a small garden,
and other implements. In short, they were as self-suf-
ficient as they could be.

After a while, Randy got to picking at the guitar
and Becky came out to speak with Cameron.

'When do you think all the trouble will be over?'
she asked tentatively.

'That's hard to say. I want you to know how much
I appreciate that you didn't say anything to Gilson
and his men.'

'What could I say? Those men are fools anyway,
and murderers.'

Her voice had changed and Cameron sensed that
she wanted to say more.

'I don't mean to pry,' he said, 'but have Gilson and
his men given you much trouble?'

She broke eye contact briefly, and then held her
gaze on his. 'They killed my husband,' she said,
'although I can't prove it.'

'I see, and I'm sorry to hear that. What I can tell

you is that those men will be accountable to the law. I promise you that.'

'I've heard that before. Sheriff Kerrigan is a good man, but he's not a fool. There's nothing he can do about Gilson and his men.'

'Time has a way of working things out.'

'That's a fancy philosophy, but I prefer facts. I have this ranch to handle, and a son to raise. My husband was killed by evil men, and nothing can change that. I can only hope that justice will prevail, but it rarely does. This is the west, and the west is a mighty brutal place.' She blushed, and broke eye contact again. 'I'm sorry. I guess I talk too much.'

'That's all right, Becky. I understand. As long as you know I'll help you any way I can.'

'That's fine, and I appreciate that. I really do. Just don't go and get yourself killed. You'll be safer if you ride on.'

Cameron smiled. 'I'll see what I can do.'

'Thank you, Cam, I really mean that.'

He watched her walk back to the cabin and disappear inside, his pulse suddenly racing a lot faster than it normally did.

He went to the bunkhouse, which turned out to be a forlorn place because it was empty. It was a warm night and he found himself feeling strangely happy. The bunkhouse had four cots, a pot-bellied stove and a stack of firewood for the coming autumn. It would be a comfortable place in the winter, or on any night after putting in a day's hard work. Each cot had a

Mexican blanket. All Becky needed was extra help, and maybe a dozen more head of cattle. This could shape up to be quite a ranch.

He sat on the cot but he wasn't tired. He thought about Randy, and the way he had taken to that guitar. He turned the oil lamp down and tried to sleep, but sleep eluded him. He slipped outside and walked quietly to the barn. Nothing was amiss. Becky and Randy were undoubtedly sleeping. The cabin was dark and silent. The warm night wind nudged him and some inner instinct told him to remain silent.

There was something in the night that bothered him.

He was conscious of the weight of his holstered Colt on his right hip. He slipped around the side of the barn and melted into the darkness. Edging along the corral fence, he surveyed the ranch from a distance of fifty yards. He had a good view, but there was no sign of intruders. He set his gaze on the surrounding countryside. Becky was a capable woman, but she was vulnerable here. Without help, she was too far from town to defend herself adequately.

He thought there was someone out there in the dark, up in the trees on one of the surrounding hills. Moving silently, he made his way toward the hills, keeping to a thin stretch of trees that offered a mosaic of jumbled shadows in the starlight.

When he was about a hundred yards from the cabin, he paused and listened, his senses alert for any movement or sound. The minutes crawled along;

and then he heard a horse snort. The sound was far up the incline and into the hills. Only his acute senses had picked up the sound. There was a man on horseback, up in the hills, watching Becky's ranch. Whoever it was undoubtedly knew he was here, and might have seen him slip out the door.

There was nothing he could do. Cameron waited patiently. He was not prone to panic like some men. He never even pulled his gun. Sometime later, he thought he heard hoofbeats, perhaps indicating the man had departed.

For Cameron Scott, instinct was everything. His eyes searched the night, taking in the lavender shadows and coal-black landscape all at once, defining each shape and assessing what he saw. The land was beautiful but treacherous, made all the deadlier by men like the Gilson family.

There might have been a gunman out in the darkness, but if there had been he'd since left. Someone had been out there, of that he was sure, but it didn't matter now. He knew who that man might have been, and the reckoning would come soon enough.

EIGHT

Montague Irving Gallant was a man who noticed things. He noticed sunsets and sunrises because he believed the color of the sky said something about the day. He noticed the sounds of wolves howling in the distance, or the clip-clop of iron-shod hoofs on a dusty trail. He noticed the look in men's eyes because he knew that look might warn him a killer had come to town. He noticed all of these things, and more, and while he might not understand all of the knowledge he accumulated by noticing things, he kept that knowledge close to himself and relied on his instinct to make sense of it.

He noticed that Larry Strickland had the look of a killer. That didn't surprise him by itself, but the fact that he was allied with Jim and Dave Gilson was reason enough to ponder it. To top it off, Cameron Scott's arrival got him to thinking about motives and coincidences.

Motives, he thought, were easy to figure out, and

he didn't believe in coincidences.

There was an evil wind blowing through the town of Willow Branch Creek, and it lingered like a festering disease. Monty Gallant, however, wasn't worried, but he was curious.

He had met Cameron Scott a long time ago, and his sudden arrival in Willow Branch Creek brought back many fond memories. Cameron was about the nicest kid Monty had ever met, but he quickly learned the kid was no pushover. He was fast and accurate with a gun and tough with his fists. He never backed down, but he also demonstrated an ability to use his head wisely. Cameron was sharp, and nobody's fool. The years hadn't changed him. If anything, he seemed calmer and nicer, if that was possible, but obviously his run-in with Drucker had proven he still had an edge. That was good. Cameron would need to stay alert with Jim Gilson and his son Dave gunning for him.

After a lunch of steak and potatoes followed by a glass of frothy beer, he ambled up to the sheriff's office and entered without knocking. Sheriff Charlie Kerrigan was at the desk sorting through a stack of Wanted posters. He glanced up at Monty and returned his attention to the posters.

'You looking for someone in particular?' Monty asked.

'Strickland.'

'That's a long shot, but I'd look, too.'

'I'm glad my effort meets with your approval.'

Monty pulled up a chair and straddled it with the back facing the sheriff, his arms over the old slatted wood.

'How do you think this is going to play out?'

'With a lot of blood,' Kerrigan said in a strong voice. He looked at Monty. 'Tell me about your friend.'

'He's resourceful. He tough, and he won't back down.'

'Sounds like a lot of men around here.'

'Thing is we don't know what he's up to.'

'Well, you know him well enough, so what do you think he's up to?'

'I reckon he's planning, thinking things over, and looking around.'

Kerrigan nodded. 'That's pretty much what I'm doing. The way I see it, that poker game is going to happen, and the train will get robbed afterward, just like the others.'

'Cameron is out to stop the robbery, and if he can he'll prove the Gilsons are involved. Sounds simple enough.'

'Men like the Gilsons won't let it be simple. Hell, Jim Gilson all by himself is a handful. With hired guns and his crazy son riding with him, there's not much that can stop him.'

'Except us.'

'Us?' Sheriff Kerrigan focused on Monty. 'Are you planning on being involved?'

'You should deputize me, make it legal.'

'Is that right? I figure we'll have one chance after the train pulls out. Do you know what I'm talking about?'

'I don't have family, and I'm not afraid to die. The good Lord will see things right.'

'I'm a widower, so I don't have family either, but this could finish us off.'

'Have you talked with Hockman and Robeson?'

'I have. They're in. I spelled it out for them. That makes four of us.'

'Five. You forgot Cameron.'

'I haven't forgotten him, but I don't know how he'll figure into this. I can't rely on him because he's not here.' Sheriff Kerrigan pulled open a desk drawer, pulled out a tin star and tossed it to Monty. 'Raise your right hand.'

Monty raised his hand.

'You're deputized.'

'That's it? Don't you say special words or anything?'

'I don't remember the oath. It goes something like, I hereby deputize you, and buy your own damn ammunition.'

Monty lowered his hand and affectionately patted the tin star he'd pinned to his vest. 'Good thing I own a gun.'

'This is going to heat up fast enough and the clock is ticking,' Kerrigan said.

'Cameron is out there, and by now he's looked over the railroad tracks. I'll bet he's figured out where the robbery will take place, so he'll be waiting.'

'I thought of that. That's rugged country. I rode out there myself, and the train slows just before Devil's Canyon. That's about sixty miles from here.'

'They'll stop the train before that, rob it, and skedaddle.'

Sheriff Kerrigan took a deep breath while considering the matter. Then he said, 'You and I have known each other a long time.' Monty nodded. 'So what I don't know is how you'll behave in a gunfight. I have no problem making you deputy, but can you shoot straight?'

Monty gave a short chuckle. 'I can, and once I start something I'll see it through to the end.'

'Don't take any offense by this, but the only thing I've known you see through to the end is a plate of steak and potatoes.'

'Don't worry about me. You've got my word on that.'

Now it was Sheriff Kerrigan's turn to nod. 'A man is only as good as his word.'

'Cameron is an honest man, Sheriff. You have my word on that, too.'

'Robeson doesn't trust him because he's a Pinkerton man.'

'What's he got against the Pinkertons?'

'He didn't say. I want you to go talk to him since you know Cameron. He might listen to you. My concern is that Robeson might shoot him when things get hot. Robeson can be a hothead at times.'

'What about Hockman?'

'He's all right. Ranching keeps him busy but he's good with a gun. He doesn't have any kind words for Gilson.'

'I'll talk to Robeson. Anything else?'

'That'll do it. Robeson is down by the stables having Amos put some new iron on his horse.'

Monty walked leisurely into the blistering sunlight. He couldn't help but think that the summer heat was one thing, but the furnace that was about to be stoked was another thing altogether.

Amos Longstreet's blacksmith business was adjacent to the stables. Monty heard the hard *kchang!* of a hammer striking the anvil as he strolled into the shadowed interior. It was humid inside rather than cooler. Amos was working the bellows to keep the fire going as the shirtless Robeson slammed his hammer onto the glowing horseshoe. Sparks flew. Sweat glistened on his forearms. Robeson was tall, muscular and possessed of a fierce temperament that Monty had seen but flashes of here and there. Still, he knew that Robeson was like a stick of dynamite, just as the sheriff had indicated.

Monty noticed that Robeson's holstered Colt was hanging over a chair just inches away. The man was prepared. Both men paused and looked up as Monty entered the blacksmith's barn.

'Howdy, Monty,' Amos said.

'Howdy.'

'When the hell did you start wearing a tin star?' Robeson asked.

'Since about ten minutes ago. I reckon you'll need help if you're going up against Gilson.'

'Is that right? We don't even know if Gilson is behind those robberies.'

'But we're all gonna find out, and I'm here to help.'

'The sheriff must be hard-up for deputies.'

'Listen, I know Cameron and he's not a bad sort. He won't be against us.'

'So you came here to tell me not to shoot him?'

'Something like that.'

Robeson slammed the hammer onto the horse-shoe with such ferocity, Monty felt the building shake.

'Damn! I hate being careful in a gunfight!'

Amos, who had been listening to this exchange with a raised eyebrow, said, 'You boys are going up against Gilson?'

'Now, Amos,' Monty said quickly, 'you're sworn to secrecy. You have to keep your mouth shut, or I'll have to ask Robeson here to kill you.'

Robeson set the hammer down and leveled his gaze at Amos. 'And I will.'

Amos swallowed hard. 'I can keep my mouth shut! The only time I have my mouth open is when I'm eating or if I'm kissing a woman over at the social club!'

'I hear that!' Monty said with a big grin.

On Friday morning the train rested on the tracks at
the depot in Willow Branch Creek, steam billowing
from the stack like angry spirits. The Indians called
the train the Iron Horse. Monty sat on a bench at the
depot chewing on some tobacco and perusing the
tons of metal, and decided a train was an amazing
invention. He understood how the coal and wood
fueled the train, but he never understood the actual
mechanical operation. The details were beyond his
scope. A horse and wagon was enough for him. He
had a vague sense that its individual parts were
forged in some faraway place like Chicago or New
York, and he wondered how many men it took to
piece it together. For Monty, the train was a marvel of
the modern age.

The businessmen from St Louis were something to
consider. They wore the finest clothes. There were
four of them, and they looked like four pompous
fools. Their damn shoes were so shiny they reflected
the sky. All four had gold watches in their pockets
and clipped to their vests with gold chains. Each
man, in turn, made a point of disembarking from the
train and checking the time on his fancy gold watch
and commenting on their schedule.

The women were young, dressed up like some
Sears & Roebuck drawing, all frills and lace and billowing skirts and parasols. Monty thought the
women at the social club looked better, but of course,

they wore fewer clothes. The women chattered like birds, their eyes flicking suspiciously toward the few locals who were ambling around the depot. When they laughed, it sounded phony, like nervous schoolkids who had done something wrong. The thought crossed Monty's mind that allowing this group of starched shirts to be robbed wasn't necessarily a bad thing.

They all disappeared into the Lucky Ace Saloon. Monty knew the routine. The men would be entertained with gambling, and when their women were appropriately distracted, they might be entertained by a special dove or two, and then more gambling. They would win at first, and then they would lose, but the distractions would more than make up for their losses. Of course, at the end of it all they would win again, because the plan was to steal the money back. If Cameron was right, and Monty believed he was, the train would be robbed and these men and their women would have real stories to tell about their time in the 'wild west'.

The afternoon proceeded without incident. Sheriff Kerrigan found Monty sitting in a rickety chair outside the barber's shop, chewing on a toothpick.

'I've got Hockman and Robeson killing time at a camp a mile outside of town. There's nothing we can do until that train pulls out.'

'I expect it's business as usual. The only thing is, I haven't seen that Strickland fellow.'

'Is that right? Well, maybe he high-tailed it.'

'I don't think so. He's in with the Gilsons now, at least as an extra gun.'

'Any sign of Cam?'

'Not a whisper. That doesn't concern me much because he'll be out on the tracks when that train leaves.'

'I don't like any of it. There's too many ways this can go wrong.'

'Maybe Cam will be the deciding factor in your favor.'

'Maybe, and maybe he'll be the reason some good men die.'

With that, the sheriff stalked away, leaving Monty to ponder the aging lawman's insistent crankiness.

Twilight settled on Willow Branch Creek and for a brief moment it was a perfect summer's day. The dark blue sky, the gentle brush of wind against the tall oaks and the late afternoon sunlight all added a sense of tranquility to the town. Only the distant raucous piano playing and outbursts of laughter from the Lucky Ace Saloon were a reminder of the deadly game they were all prepared to play.

Monty dozed off, and when he next opened his eyes it was just after dark and the oil lamps were starting to throw shadows at the lavender night. A horse neighed to his right, and as he blinked and looked up he saw Strickland on horseback cantering into town. He kept his head low to feign sleeping but lifted one surreptitious eyelid to mark his progress.

Strickland lashed his horse to the hitching post near the Lucky Ace Saloon and went inside.

Monty went to the sheriff's office, but the lights were out and the door was locked. Hell, that makes sense, he thought. It was when those greenhorns from St. Louis took the train home that things would heat up. He decided to cash it in for the night and hit his bunk hard. All of this anticipation had tuckered him out.

But before that, he wanted one last look around. He decided to see things for himself so he ambled into the Lucky Ace Saloon as nonchalantly as he could, and swigged a foamy beer at the bar. Nobody paid any attention to him. Both Gilsons were at a corner table playing poker with their own ranch hands, which was unusual but not illegal. Strickland was nowhere to be seen. The boys from St. Louis appeared to be having a fine time. The air was heavy with cigar smoke, laughter, the piano playing and the occasional whiff of some harlot's perfume.

Monty finished his beer, pushed off the stool and went out. The street was quiet, and most of the windows were dark. He couldn't get to his old bunk at Lorraine's Boarding House fast enough. Tomorrow was going to a big day.

Less than a minute after Monty had exited the Lucky Ace Saloon, Strickland struck a wood matchstick against his denim and lit his cheroot. The burning tobacco cast a yellow glow across his cruel features after Monty had passed the dark alley where he had been hiding since sneaking out the rear entrance. His cold, dark eyes were emotionless as he watched Monty amble up the street.

NINE

Jim Gilson had a bellyful of whiskey. He didn't take anything for granted, and after playing poker he was satisfied that everything was in place. That gunslinger Cameron Scott had taken it for granted that he would win. The sheriff had done the same. Those two fools camped outside of town had made the identical miscalculation, and that fat fool, Monty, had done the same. Jim Gilson had never taken anything for granted, and he was confident all of those men would die.

Of course, it was dangerous having the sheriff killed, but it had to be done. Killing a lawman was playing the game hard, but Sheriff Charlie Kerrigan had doomed himself. Gilson would see to it that the sheriff died first, then that damn Pinkerton agent Cameron Scott.

Gilson had a surprise lined up for all of them on that train.

A surprise that included ten extra gunmen in two

freight cars, with horses.

Strickland had come in handy, although Gilson wasn't foolish enough to trust him completely. The man took advantage of opportunities, and his connection to the Pinkerton man had proven useful. Still, he was prepared to shoot him immediately if the need arose. On this matter, he remained reticent, keeping such a thought to himself. His foolish son Dave had taken a liking to the man, which irked the elder Gilson somewhat.

He was alone in his den, the whiskey on the desk in front of him. Sleep was impossible. Events had spiraled out of control, and somehow he had to piece together the fragments of his life or risk losing everything.

The thought briefly crossed his mind that it didn't really matter. He had already lost. He had lost and been lost since his beloved wife died, and his sons had earned the reputation of being saddle-tramp scum. Now Steve was dead and Dave was nearly a stranger to him.

Where had it all gone wrong?

The whiskey slid down his throat burning like fire. Then the warmth blossomed in his belly and he felt almost normal again. It was taking more whiskey nowadays to get that warm feeling and make it last, but whiskey was readily available.

Damn that guitar-playing Pinkerton man.

He comes into town with an easy manner all friendly-like, a winning smile for the widow Drake, and then he kills Steve saying he had no choice.

He eyes fell upon the brass-framed daguerreotype of his wife. His memory of her was like silver moonlight and assuaged him of the guilt of his sins, the madness of his actions, and the folly of his sons. He occasionally clung to such memories, nearly reveling in them in his whiskey-laced stupor, but no matter how hard he tried something in the memory was always twisted. So he drank. The horrifying visage of his wife's maggot-infested corpse rising like a specter from the earth, her tattered gown blowing in the evil breeze, the jaws of her grinning skull chattering with a sound like castanets, all filled him with unspeakable horror. Small ravens fluttering in her long hair, their dark wings flapping as if her head had become a nest for a generation of eggs to hatch; the pungent sulfur odor assailing him. At such moments Gilson was frozen in abject terror, his muscles constricted and his mouth dry as cotton.

There were times when he considered putting the Colt to his head.

He drank, nearly guzzling the whiskey like a man starved for water in the Mohave. He recalled his wife telling him, 'Don't be so hard on the boys!' It was true he had driven them hard, because that was the only way they'd learn anything. If he had been too hard on them, then so be it! She was gone now anyway, so what did it matter? What did anything matter?

The Pinkerton man had killed Steve, and there

had to be vengeance. That was the way of things here in the west. A man made his own law.

He finished the bottle of whiskey and pushed himself out of the chair. He felt his age catching up with him, although he wasn't all that old. He pulled the chain of his pocket watch, slipping it from his pocket and into his palm, and flipped open the cover. Past midnight. That was when the demons always came to visit him. He stared at the oval daguerreotype of his late wife in the pocket-watch case. So pretty. Still young. That was the year she had married him.

The ranch was quiet, too quiet.

He wandered out on the porch. There was no moon, and he felt dizzy when he glanced up at the scattering of stars. The yellow glow of an oil lamp in the bunkhouse window cast an eerie glow along the fence-line. All else was darkness. He could hear the leaves high in the oaks muttering in the breeze.

There were voices in the bunkhouse, and laughter. Nothing unusual there. He heard one of the men singing drunkenly, '. . . Open up your corset and show me your stuff, I've got a pocket full of money and I'm feelin' kind of rough. . . .' The other men chortled and guffawed.

A sound in the distance caught his attention. Moving away from the window, Gilson ambled toward the barn. There was a small shed on the right side and he slipped into the darkest place between the barn and the shed.

He had heard the clip-clop of a horse coming along the trail.

Presently, a rider came into view, but it was too dark to see who it was. The rider dismounted and led his horse into the barn. Gilson waited, curious as to which of his ranch hands had been out at this late hour.

When the figure emerged from the barn he recognized Strickland's profile as he made his way toward the bunkhouse. He was only slightly surprised that Strickland had been away. The man was odd, and untrustworthy. Gilson had no doubt that Strickland harbored his own plans that were designed to benefit only himself. Gilson decided to confront him.

Strickland had his hand on the bunkhouse door when Gilson called out.

'Hold on, Strickland!'

Wheeling about, Strickland let his hand drop to his holster.

'Boss, you startled me! I didn't see you standing there!'

'I didn't intend on you seeing me. Now tell me, where have you been?'

'Just out snooping. Dave and I talked and he thought I might nosy around for any sign of the Pinkerton man.'

'So, did you learn anything?'

'He was out at the Drake ranch. She's a pretty thing and I suppose he might fancy her. I like the way

106

she fills out a shirt myself.'

'How long did he stay?'

'He rode out at sunup. He stayed in the bunkhouse, did some chores. I lost his trail in the hills.'

'And the others?'

'No change. Hockman and Robeson are camped outside of town. The sheriff keeps to himself but he's been talking to that fat old man.'

'Monty. He's a friend of the Pinkerton man.'

'That won't help him later.'

'No, it won't.

'Now you listen carefully to me, Strickland. I've put my life into this operation. This guitar-playing Pinkerton man is no fool. He killed Steve fast enough. Don't be fooled by that guitar. He's quick with a gun and resourceful. We've gone looking for him but come up empty, so he knows how to use the land to his advantage.'

'I can vouch for his resourcefulness, boss.'

'So you said. That scar he gave you is good enough reason to want some revenge, but don't get overconfident.'

'He's still only one man, and a lonesome man at that. Why, he isn't any better than any skyline rider looking for a home. He sure has the widow Drake eating from his hand!'

Gilson ran his hand over his jaw. 'That gives me an idea. Tell me more about what you saw. You say he spent the night in the bunkhouse?'

'That he did. The night before he had dinner with the woman and her boy. I heard them laughing and singing. This morning he helped the boy with his chores. They all get along like a family.'

Gilson nodded, thinking hard. 'All right, so this is what I'm going to do, and you're gonna help. I want you at the ranch when we stop the train.'

'But boss, you promised I'd have a chance at killing Cameron Scott!'

'Ease up, and pay attention! Scott's clever, and we won't take him down easily. When things heat up we'll need another option. You're a gambler, so you know how it is. Be prepared for anything. You'll have your revenge on Scott, and that woman is a bonus I'm giving you. This is what I want you to do. . . .'

TEN

Sheriff Charlie Kerrigan was surprised to find Cameron Scott sitting in an old maple chair with his boots propped up on the hitching post outside of his office.

'Good morning, Sheriff.'

'Where the hell have you been?'

'Me? Why, Sheriff, you told me ride on. Are you saying you're happy to see me?'

The sheriff cursed and glowered at Scott. 'What kind of game are you playing here? I'm only half surprised that you're still alive.'

'Like I said before, Sheriff, this sure is an unfriendly town. Why don't we step into your office to talk things over. We wouldn't want the gossip to start if folks see me resting my spurs this early in the morning.'

The sheriff led him into the office where Cameron made himself comfortable in another chair. The sheriff went to work heating up coffee on the stove.

When the coffee was hot he filled a tin cup for each of them, stationed himself at his desk and studied Cameron through the steam rising from his cup.

'Start talking.'

'I'll be straight with you. I know the place where Gilson and his men plan on stopping the train. I'll be there. If you can have your men ride in, then we can take them quickly and put an end to this whole thing.'

'You can't be so stupid to believe it will be that easy.'

'No, I don't. I believe a fast and firm approach will give us the best odds for success. I'll be on that train. I've already spoken with the engineer, and I'll ride with him, and climb over the coal car once they're underway.'

'I see. So once the train stops we can ride down and take on Gilson and his men, hopefully before they even get aboard to rob the passengers.'

'That seems reasonable to me.'

'You'll be alone on that train with a six-gun in your holster. It doesn't matter how fast you are with a gun; you'll be outnumbered if they board that train.'

'I'll take that chance.'

'Gilson knows you're here, and he knows you'll try something. He's like a rattlesnake. Fast and deadly. I think you're a damn fool.'

Cameron nodded. 'Maybe I am. We have to try.'

Sheriff Kerrigan sipped his coffee. 'I'm holding you responsible. If any passengers are injured or killed, then I'm putting you in jail for interfering with the law. If any of my men get killed, I might shoot you myself.'

'Sheriff, what choice do we have? Gilson is a law-breaker. Why, he's probably responsible for the death of Becky Drake's husband.'

'Damn it! I know that. I don't like this, that's all. Gilson is one hot-headed man and without mercy. He wasn't always that way, but he's changed. He won't hesitate to kill, and I guarantee that.'

'Your men are capable, and I don't see any other way.'

'There is no other way, and that fact doesn't sit right with me. I hope I'm wrong, but we'll have our hands full later this afternoon.'

'My gun is always loaded.' Cameron said.

All that day, Sheriff Kerrigan pondered his fate. He'd been a lawman for close to thirty-five years, and he was getting old. He knew it didn't matter much to anyone if he took a bullet or not, but he was worried about Hockman and Robeson. They were tough men, but they had families. He wouldn't tolerate seeing them killed or crippled. As for Monty, the man was amiable and honest, and he didn't need to die uselessly. The problem was, they were all he had.

As far as he was concerned, Cameron Scott was the unknown factor. The man had a way about him that inspired confidence, but they also needed some luck.

Sitting in his office and drinking coffee didn't do him much good, but he figured he had no choice.

There was nothing to do but watch the long stretch of shadows as the sun moved across the afternoon sky.

Once an hour he'd get up, stroll out to the board-walk and smoke, and then return to his desk and sip his coffee.

If everything went according to schedule, the St. Louis gamblers would depart the saloon at four o'clock that afternoon and board the train for a departure twenty minutes later.

Sheriff Kerrigan had plenty of reasons to worry. They had attempted to stop the train robbery before, but their plans had become known and it had resulted in the murder of deputy Jason Drake. His death had caused more grief than God should allow on earth. It wasn't right that Cameron might have given Becky Drake some hope that justice would be served. The situation had spiraled out of control.

The afternoon dragged on, and then at four o'clock that afternoon he stood on the depot plat-form and watched the St. Louis boys and their women board the train. They all looked tired but content, oblivious to the orchestrated events tran-spiring around them.

Monty was sitting on a bench nearby, arms crossed over his chest. There was no sign of Gilson or any of his men, although Sheriff Kerrigan figured they were on board.

'You ready?'

'I reckon so,' Monty said. 'Let's get to it.'

112

Cameron pulled himself up into the engineer's cage and smiled. The engineer was a man named Otto with bushy eyebrows and a healthy belly that hung over his belt. His shirt was stained from chewing tobacco that had difficulty making it past his lower lip when he spat. Cameron had introduced himself earlier.

'We about ready to go?' Cameron asked.

'That we are, but with some extras since the last time we talked.'

'How so?'

'Mister Gilson put ten men with horses in two boxcars. He says he's gonna help protect the train.'

Cameron took the news stoically. 'When did they board?'

'About fifteen minutes ago. So is being a Pinkerton man like being a bounty hunter?'

'No, it's not the same. Can I borrow that shotgun?'

Cameron pointed to the sawed-off double-bar-reled twelve gauge propped in the corner.

'I expect that'll be fine. There's extra shells down in that foot-locker.'

Cameron retrieved the extra shells and stuffed them in his vest pocket. He clicked open the breech and there were two shells already loaded.

'We'll see what happens,' Cameron said with a friendly smile.

Otto's assistant was a short but stocky youth named

Andy who clambered onto the train a few moments later to help shovel coal into the fire. The two men took turns and they built up a head of steam by shoveling coal into the furnace. Cameron stepped down onto the boardwalk and watched the St Louis visitors board the train. There was no sign of Gilson or his son. He noted the two cattle cars where undoubtedly Gilson's men were waiting. Once the train left Willow Branch Creek they would travel about forty-five minutes before the train would be stopped and robbed.

Otto and Andy bantered back and forth, with Otto doing most of the talking. The coach carrying the passengers was the first after the coal car, followed by a freight car, two cattle cars, and a caboose. A man named Alfred rode the caboose; a weathered old-timer according to Otto who claimed to have met Abe Lincoln at Gettysburg.

With steam churning in its iron belly, the train whistled and whined, lurched forward and rattled to life. For Cameron, a train was a marvel of industry; a beast made of steel tonnage, noisy and irritating but truly a far more comfortable way to travel across the west for those with money to afford such a luxury.

'I'll see you boys in a bit,' he said to Otto and Andy.

'Watch who you're calling a boy,' Otto said, beaming, his face already drenched in sweat.

Cameron picked his way carefully across the coal car and climbed over the railing onto the coach plat-

114

form. He opened the door and walked in; a brazen act, but he felt he needed to be bold if he was going to succeed. Keeping the shotgun held low at his left side with one hand, his goal wasn't to alarm the passengers but to reassure them. The surprise that greeted him, however, was the fact that Gilson and his son were not aboard the coach. In fact, none of Gilson's men were riding in the coach.

At the sight of him entering the coach, exclamations of surprise and concern rose up from the passengers.

'What's the meaning of this?' one of the St. Louis men said, eying the shotgun in his hand.

'Easy now, folks,' Cameron said with an easy smile. 'My name is Cameron Scott and I work for the Pinkerton Agency. I'm helping provide security for your ride home.'

'That sounds like you're expecting trouble.'

'There might be a little trouble along the rails, but nothing to be concerned about. Now does anyone know where Mister Gilson went off to?'

'Why, he's back in the freight car,' one man said. 'He told us not to worry about a thing. I'm certainly impressed by the level of security afforded us.'

'Well, everyone can take it easy and not worry. I'm just looking things over.'

With that, Cameron exited the opposite end of the coach and stood on the platform connecting to the freight car. There was no window in the door, and for whatever reason Gilson had decided to stay out of

115

sight, but at least Cameron knew where he was. He was concerned about the ten gunmen in the cattle cars. It had to be hot and smelly in those cars with those horses, and those men would be happy for a fight.

The door opened abruptly and one of Gilson's men was startled to find Cameron standing before him. He went for his holstered gun, cursing, as Cameron flipped the shotgun up and slammed the stock into the man's jaw. He kicked the man backward and sent him sprawling onto the floor.

Inside the coach, Jim Gilson and his son Dave were sitting at a table with a bottle of whiskey in front of them. They had been playing cards. Cameron leveled the shotgun on the two men, equally surprised by the sudden turn of events.

'Easy does it. We should be stopping soon so your robbery can happen.'

Cameron saw it in their eyes. A hatred so pure it clouded their judgment. He saw it coming, and he knew their reactions perhaps before they did.

'You hurt Eric here real bad,' Jim Gilson said.

Eric, moaning on the floor and holding his busted jaw, quickly lashed out and kicked Cameron in the legs, throwing him off balance. The Gilsons were on their feet, guns drawn, and Cameron let go with one barrel that went high as he lurched backward out the door.

Twisting to the side, he slammed the door as bullets shattered the wood, missing him by inches.

The sound of gunfire was muted by the rumble of the train as it turned a bend on the narrow tracks.

Cameron rushed through the coach where the startled passengers were all shouting questions at him. There was no time to placate them. One of the passengers stood up and blocked his path.

'Here now! What's this all about? You said there was nothing to worry. . . .'

Cameron shoved him back into his seat and exited the coach. Immediately, he mounted the exterior railing, pulling himself onto the roof. There was little time before the proposed robbery brought the train to a stop. The unexpected and unwanted encounter with Gilson added a sense of urgency to his actions.

They would be gunning for him now.

The wind buffeted him as the roar of the steam engine and the clatter of iron wheels drowned out all sound. Staying near the edge above the platform seemed like the safest place, especially knowing they would come at him from both sides.

The gunman named Eric came first, his head appearing on the far side. He had come right up the railing and was pulling himself onto the coach's roof when Cameron let loose with the right barrel. The blast tore into Eric, flinging him loose. With an agonized yell, he plummeted from the train. Cameron saw his body tumbling onto the rocky earth trailing a fountain of crimson.

For a moment all he heard was the clatter of the steel wheels and then the door opened below him.

117

He had one glimpse of the gunman as the man glanced up, swinging his Colt to aim at Cameron. The second barrel's blast flipped the man backward and off the train as well. Cameron slid from the roof, and craned his neck to look into the passenger coach.

His ears rang from the noise of the gunfire. He sensed a blur of motion, like a piece of grit caught in the eye; something that made its presence known but wasn't visible. His instincts were right and he heeded the alarm bells that racketed in his brain. He threw himself down just as a shot sounded, the bullet's impact shattering the wood paneling in the doorway. The passengers were screaming in fear.

His assailant's gun barked again; an ugly percussive pop that filled the air with the pungent scent of gunsmoke. He was crouched behind the door, but he knew the man was only ten feet away, crouched in the aisle behind a seat. Cameron didn't want to take any unnecessary chances with the passengers in the line of fire. He had to draw the man out to get a clear shot.

The train was slowing.

He cracked open the shotgun, shook out the spent shells, and plunged two fresh shells into the breech.

He heard shouts out on the tracks as the train slowed to a crawl. He left the gunman in the coach and went over the coal car to climb back onto the engineer's box. Up ahead a massive bonfire was raging. Cut timber had been piled high, blocking the tracks. Four riders with their faces covered by bandannas framed the burning timber. Otto and Andy and were watching the riders with interest.

'I reckon this'll be a showdown,' Andy said.

'It'll be something,' Otto said, 'especially with Mister Gilson's men back there. This should be something to see.' Otto looked at Cameron. 'What was all that shootin' about?'

'Oh, I was just practising is all.'

Otto and Andy looked confused but didn't say anything else. Cameron slipped off the train and went hustling toward the caboose. A quick look around for the sheriff failed to reassure him of anything.

He didn't get far.

The two car doors slid open and the riders began to disembark. The riders out front were cantering in his direction. Cameron was stuck between the two groups of Gilson's men. He slid between the coal car and the passenger coach, looking for a better vantage point. The thought crossed his mind that Gilson had outsmarted them all. He had the upper hand with a sizeable force of men.

A volley of gunfire erupted from the train where the riders were dropping from the freight car. A shot winged past him.

Too close. The bullet nearly clipped his ear. He heard it buzzing in the air.

Dave Gilson had jumped from the train and was pointing his Colt in Cameron's direction. His face was plastered with a malicious grin.

Cameron spun, dropped to one knee as he pulled his six-shooter from its holster with his free hand, and fired.

The bullet burst into Dave Gilson's gun arm, just above the elbow. He shrieked, the gun falling from his numb fingers. Holstering his Colt, Cameron locked the shotgun bead on Gilson and said, 'Where's your father?'

Dave Gilson cursed, calling Cameron vile names.

'That isn't very nice.'

'You're gonna die! You hear me? You ain't got a chance!'

Gunfire echoed across the tracks and they heard men shouting.

Cameron kicked Gilson's dropped six-shooter away, and in one swift movement he slammed the shotgun stock into the side of Gilson's head, knocking him instantly unconscious. With Dave Gilson incapacitated, he set to the task of locating Jim Gilson.

He needed to end this quickly.

ELEVEN

In a flurry of dust and wild gunfire, Gilson's men had disembarked and began a mad gallop around the stalled train. With their bandanas pulled over their faces, it became clear that Gilson's purpose was to put on a show of force intended to bushwhack Cameron while still succeeding in robbing the train. A distant echo of gunfire reinforced Cameron's hunch that Sheriff Kerrigan and the other men were counter-attacking. A rider, having circled the train, emerged from the billowing clouds of steam and leveled his gun on Cameron.

Bringing the shotgun, up, Cameron let loose with both barrels. The force knocked him backward, but he remained on his feet. The rider went down in a swirl of dust, his horse bucking and then sprinting away. He had just had time to slip two fresh cartridges into the breech when another rider descended on him. This time, he discharged one barrel, and the rider twisted in agony, clutching his side. The sound of gunfire echoed across the hills.

Cameron slipped between the steam engine and the coal car, ducked under and emerged on the other side. The scene he witnessed was pure chaos. Several riders were circling and firing in the air; apparently an act to frighten the passengers into submission. More riders were engaged in a running gun battle with Sheriff Kerrigan and the other men who had taken up a flanking position in a nearby copse of trees.

He only had a glimpse of Hockman and Robeson, stationed about fifty yards from each other. His brief glimpse of the sheriff was obscured by the dust the horses were kicking up. Of his friend Monty, he saw nothing, but he knew his loyal friend was in the thick of it.

Bracing himself, he raced ahead, and kicked a man between the legs. The man lurched forward, dropping to his knees, and vomited before rolling on his side while holding his groin and wailing in agony.

Some inner instinct made him turn just as an outlaw on foot lashed at him with a knife. With a shock, Cameron realized it was Jim Gilson.

'Come on, boy! You're gonna bleed!'

The knife swept toward him and Cameron slipped sideways to avoid its sting. Gilson's eyes were gleaming. Cameron functioned from instinct and experience. He circled Gilson, dodging the knife. He wouldn't shoot him, and Gilson seemed to sense this. Cameron wanted Gilson alive, and in jail.

'I had this all planned,' Gilson gloated. 'My men are protecting the passengers from being robbed by you and the crooked sheriff! Don't you see? I've thought of everything!'

In his peripheral vision, Cameron saw Sheriff Kerrigan on foot and coming toward them.

'Too bad your plan failed,' Cameron said. 'The sheriff here would like to talk to you about all of this.'

Gilson paused, glancing over his shoulder. 'You're too late, Sheriff! My men have you outnumbered!'

The sheriff came up with his gun drawn.

'Drop the knife, Gilson, it's over. I'll shoot you down if you don't call your men back.'

Gilson was like a wounded, trapped animal. 'I should have killed you when I killed your deputy!'

'You can tell that to the judge before he sentences you to hang.'

Gilson spun around and angrily faced Cameron again. 'You think you're so smart? Let me tell you about the plans your old friend Strickland has for that woman and her son!' Gilson saw the surprise in Cameron's face. 'That's right! I sent him to her ranch! You know how hungry men handle a fresh woman don't you, boy!'

Cameron used the shotgun stock to knock Gilson senseless. The sheriff then handcuffed him, pulled him to his feet and slapped him across the face to bring him around.

'Let's get him up into the train and we can have the engineer get us back to town.'

They were pulling Gilson up onto the passenger car when a hail of gunfire erupted, the bullets careening off the train. In the flurry of dust and pandemonium, some of Gilson's men had seen them and were trying to rescue their boss.

Cameron put the shotgun to Gilson's head and shouted for them to stop, but his words fell on deaf ears. The men were in a frenzy, and they were also confused.

For a moment they were pinioned on the platform between coaches as the hot lead ricocheted around them. Sheriff Kerrigan's arm was grazed by a bullet. Taking advantage of the confusion, Gilson placed his cuffed hands on the railing and kicked the sheriff from the platform. He twisted about in a violent rage, and with his fists clenched together he used his hands as a club and pummeled Cameron as he was trying to sight the shotgun on a rider.

With a curse, Gilson leapt from the train and disappeared into the swirling dust. Cameron dropped the shotgun, but pulled his Colt and fired once after Gilson's fleeing figure. Grabbing the sheriff by the arm, he pulled the wounded lawman onto the platform and into the coach as another volley of gunfire boomed in the air.

Cameron had to act, Gilson's harsh words still ringing in his ears.

'*You know how hungry men handle a fresh woman don't you, boy!*'

Somehow, he had to get to the Skyline Ranch.

He was off the train and running without a word to the sheriff.

Rushing through the dust, he came across Hockman on horseback, his Winchester's muzzle smoking.

'I damn near shot you!' Hockman bellowed.

'The sheriff's wounded,' Cameron explained. 'He's on the train. Gilson and his men are going to ambush Becky Drake at the Skyline Ranch. I need a horse and some men to follow me.'

'Those god-awful devils!'

Hockman reined his horse around, his Winchester blazing as he rode head-on toward some of Gilson's men who were still whooping and firing on the train. A man tumbled from his horse and Cameron ran toward the stallion. Leaping into the saddle, he grabbed the reins and spurred the horse toward Hockman.

'This is finished here,' Cameron said, 'Find Robeson and Monty and meet me at the ranch.'

Before Hockman could utter a response, Cameron sank the spurs into the horse and was gone in a gallop.

TWELVE

Becky was awake before sunrise, as was her habit, but this morning was different. She possessed an uncanny intuition that never failed her, and as she went about the chores collecting the eggs from the chickens and then milking the cow, she sensed a change in the air that mingled with her feelings of apprehension. Outwardly, there was nothing different about the day, but events were playing out, this she knew, and the result would undoubtedly affect her, although she knew not how.

She had brought her late husband's Winchester with her. That finely honed instinct had spoken to her to be wary, and so she was. Maybe it was nothing; maybe it was just having these emotions riled up, especially since Cameron Scott had come to town. The Pinkerton man had made quite an unforgettable impression, and with his presence had come a sense of hope. She had no firm faith that he alone

126

could achieve a lasting peace in the valley, but he certainly represented the possibility for change. That alone, she thought, was profound.

She was cautious in considering such things. Her husband had been such a man; kind and faithful, possessed of goodwill, and a believer in justice. Now his body rested beneath the summer grass, his wooden cross already showing signs of wear.

She could hear Randy inside the ranch house picking at that guitar. He had taken to that guitar like a duck takes to water. He was changing, but not in the usual way that boys change when they grow up. His father's death had struck him like a thunderbolt, and until now he had been mostly sullen, often downright angry and bitter; his childhood had been taken from him. Then Cameron came along with that easy smile and a guitar. Suddenly, Randy was enthusiastic again, and there was a brightness in his eyes she had not seen for a long time. She took such joy herself in seeing her son happy.

She decided to stay near the house, and she instructed Randy to stay close by. There was fence-line to check, but that could wait. She knew the train had come to town, and that meant trouble. Randy would be content to pick at the guitar, and the chores she could easily handle.

By mid-morning there had been no activity; nothing unusual had occurred. Once, she thought she heard a horse neigh up in the forested hills, so she stayed near the barn and studied the landscape

127

for a few minutes. There was nothing.

That morning her ranch was infused with a gentle light; the golden morning was as fresh and peaceful as any summer morning could ever be. For a lingering moment she basked in the warm memories of her childhood; and then holding dear those few touching years when her husband was alive and her son but an infant. How wicked time's sting had torn at her!

She was pulling the bucket from the well when he spoke, startling her.

'You are something to look at, that's a fact!'

She spun around to face Larry Strickland, who had crept up from behind the barn.

'What are you doing here?' She blurted the question hastily, knowing as she said the words what was happening. Strickland stood there looking at her, but making no outward hostile move. He appeared supremely confident in his manner and tone of voice, which infuriated her all the more.

'A man likes a pretty thing like you for a lot of reasons,' he said. 'Your new friend likes you, and you like him. Ain't that sweet. It's sort of like a storybook.'

Her rifle was propped against the well, just three feet away. Her eyes instinctively swept over the rifle as she thought of it, but Strickland was no fool. Suddenly his gun was free of the holster, the barrel pointed at her belly.

'Be sensible. There's no doctor close enough to

save you if I shoot you, and I don't want to shoot you, but I will. Leave that rifle where it is.'

'What are you going to do?'

'We expect that singing cowboy saddle-tramp to come this way at some point, and I'm gonna kill him.'

'You'll never get away with this!'

'That's not for you to worry about.' He gestured with his gun-hand. 'Let's go up to the house and sit down with the boy.'

Becky's mind was racing. The house was silent. Had Randy heard Strickland talking? They went up the steps and Becky gently pushed the door open. The guitar was lying on the table. The house was empty. Strickland pushed Becky further into the room, irritated.

'Where's that damn boy go?'

What she did next surprised her, and forever after she was grateful that she had taken the chance. On her left resting on the oak bureau was the washbasin, half full of cold water. She scooped it into her hands and slammed it onto Strickland's head. The washbasin shattered, and they were both showered in fragments of the basin and the water. Strickland grunted, dropping to his knees.

Becky was like a whirlwind. She knew the distance and she knew it would be close. Rushing out the door, and with her left hand swinging it shut behind her, she was sprinting for the rifle. She would not stop. She said to herself she would rather die than give in to such a monster. She expected Strickland's bullet to strike at any second. She was running and leaping forward and had the rifle in her hand just as a bullet slammed into the well's clay side.

Crouching low, she levered a round into the Winchester, swung up and fired at the doorway, levered another round and fired again. The bullets shattered wood, missing Strickland, but he cursed and dodged to safety inside the house.

That's fine, she thought, *that mangy cur isn't going to hurt anybody today!*

Leaping up, she ran toward the barn and slipped down the side without incident. Strickland was still cursing inside the house.

She had to find Randy. She had no doubt that he was safe, and obviously having seen what was happening he had taken cover. Had he thought to take his father's Peacemaker from the bureau drawer?

Either way, Strickland wasn't going to succeed. None of them would succeed. She knew deep in her heart that Cameron would survive whatever gunfight was happening, and he would find her. Strickland had said as much himself.

All she had to do was wait, and waiting was what she planned on with one exception. If Strickland showed his face at any time she wouldn't hesitate to shoot him. No sooner did she have this thought when she saw Gilson and some of his men riding down the hill toward the ranch.

*

A mile away, Cameron Scott sat astride his horse and listened to the gunfire coming from Becky's ranch. Monty, Hockman and Robeson had come alongside him.

'I'm going in on foot from behind the ranch house,' Cameron said. 'I'll circle around and see what's what.'

'We need to hurry,' Monty said. 'Gilson is desperate now.'

Hockman, pulling his rifle from the saddle scabbard, squinted down the trail. 'Gilson is still wearing handcuffs. That will slow him down but it won't stop him. I'll swing around and come in from the east; there's scrub I can use for cover.'

'I reckon I'll ride in from the south,' Robeson mused, lighting a thin cigar. 'We'll need to be careful we don't catch each other in a crossfire.'

With their course of action decided upon, the men separated. Cameron went on foot, moving swiftly down a deer trail and circling downhill toward the ranch. He listened intently but there was no further gunfire. Once he heard voices raised in alarm, coming from the ranch. They were men's voices, probably Gilson and his men. What caused their shouting was unknown. He pushed on, nearly running.

At the bottom of a hill he slid into a cluster of short pine and birch trees to take a look. There were horses at the ranch, but only one man visible on horseback. After a moment, Gilson came out of the ranch cursing. Cameron couldn't make out all the words, but it was obvious that Becky and Randy had escaped.

Strickland came out of the ranch, his face flushed red. Gilson cursed at him. Cameron watched them walk to the barn where Strickland fetched a hammer and chisel and split the handcuff chain. With his hands free, Gilson could now handle a gun better. Gilson's men appeared, apparently after searching for Becky and Randy. Cameron could hear Gilson shouting: 'They're here somewhere! A hundred in gold to the man that brings me the woman!'

The men spread out again, dispersing in different directions. Cameron's goal now was to find Becky and Randy.

He slunk away, following his original course to come around behind the ranch house. He visualized the area in his mind. About a hundred yards behind the ranch, and up near a forested hilly section, was the grave of Becky's husband. There was a white picket fence around the small plot. The hills that rose up behind that were all part of her ranch, but this unused section was mostly timber. She must have gone that way, and he surmised that Randy was probably with her. Either way, both of them would have recognized they stood a good chance of keeping hidden up in those hills. Still, if that were the case, it wouldn't take Gilson and his men long to track them. They were on foot, and they were outnumbered.

Gunfire boomed down near the ranch. Monty,

Hockman and Robeson had started the dance. He had started up the trail when he heard the horses galloping toward him.

He turned in time to see a man raise a rifle. He jumped sideways into a clump of scrub-brush. His Colt was in his hand and he fired. The shot hit the man in the chest and tumbled him from his horse. Reacting quickly, Cameron ran to the man as the death spasm shook his body. He removed the man's holster and gun and took his Winchester.

Another man on horseback was galloping near and Cameron sent a rifle shot in his direction. Several men on foot were converging from either side. He dashed uphill and took cover in a jig-sawed cluster of birch trees.

The sudden silence was nerve-wracking. The man on horseback had disappeared. The men on foot were out of sight but undoubtedly coming after him.

He had but a moment to take a breath when a man leapt from the bushes and slammed into him. The man threw a hard punch that rattled his teeth. Cameron gripped the rifle firmly and swung it forward. The blow knocked teeth loose and left a bloody gash across the man's lips. Cameron was forced to shoot as the man pulled his gun from his holster.

Cameron didn't like the idea that he was suddenly surrounded. He took the first man's Colt and removed the cartridges from the belt, replacing the empty loops on his own holster. Tossing the holster aside, he then made certain all three guns were loaded. He stuck the two extra Peacemakers in his belt and then reloaded the rifle.

His best chance now rested on the fact that he was heavily armed. Staying out of someone's gunsight was the challenge.

He could hear Gilson's men talking in low voices. Even with his guns and the cover the forest offered, Cameron was still in grave danger. A sense of urgency spurred him into action. He had to find Becky and Randy.

Pushing through bushes, he crept along until he was closer to the voices. As quietly as possible, he parted the branches and peered out. Crouching down, he fired the rifle. The bullet tore a man's shoulder apart, and he yelped in anguish. The other man wheeled around and fired, causing Cameron to dodge low. He managed to get another rifle shot off and scamper backward.

Moving sideways, he looked out again. The man he had shot was bleeding heavily and cursing; his wound was serious and he was done for. The other man had slipped off to the left and was desperately scanning around for Cameron.

They saw each other at the same time.

Eyes widening at the sight of Cameron, the man fired quickly but the shot was wide, ripping into the greenery on Cameron's right. Cameron's Winchester barked and he thought he had hit the man in the leg before he was forced to slip away as the man levered two rounds in his direction.

A split second later a fusillade of hot lead cut apart the bushes where he had been crouched.

The gunfire had caught the attention of Gilson's other men. Cameron heard a horse neigh and men shouting. They were converging on him swiftly and he had yet to crest the hill in search of Becky.

Jumping to his feet, he ran uphill, dodging between brush and trees just as a burst of gunfire ripped up the ground near his boots. A blast of fire from several Winchesters echoed loudly through the greenery.

He was running out of time. He had to break free or the men surrounding him would trap him on the hillside.

One of Gilson's men had taken a chance and spurred his horse uphill. Sensing his pursuer, Cameron stopped, squinting down the rifle barrel. He pulled the trigger as the man aimed his Colt, but much too late. Cameron's rifle bucked once, twice; two neat shots that crashed into the man's chest, toppling him.

The woodlands had gone silent. A faint breeze teased the leaves, offering a false sense of tranquility.

Behind him another gunman came up the trail. Cameron fired quickly. The man yowled in pain, and stumbled backward. Cameron's next bullet dropped him in a crimson heap.

A second later he heard a volley of gunfire coming from the ranch.

'Cam!'

Becky's voice rang out and he spun around. She had come out of the brush and saw him standing in the deer trail. She rushed toward him with a Winchester in her hands. He resisted the urge to crush her to his chest with a strong embrace.

'Cam! Thank God you're here! We need to find Randy!'

'Do you have any idea where he's gone?'

'No, but we have to find him quickly!' There was a steely gleam in her eyes that gave him pause. 'Then we're going to take Gilson and his men to jail, or bury them, whichever they prefer!'

With that, she spun on her heels and motioned for him to follow.

THIRTEEN

Monty, Hockman and Robeson had swiftly engaged Gilson and his men in a cat-and-mouse gunfight. Monty lost sight of Hockman and Robeson almost immediately and found himself scrambling for cover in the brush near the corral. With bullets whizzing past him, he cursed himself for being overweight. A thinner man might hug the ground a little tighter than he was capable of doing.

Moving as fast as his girth allowed, he was forced to retreat a considerable distance from the house. His pulse was racing, throbbing in his ears like a drunken trombone player on the fourth of July. Inspired to be as tough as Hockman and Robeson, and eager to assist his old friend Cameron, Monty leapt up and dashed along a trail littered with pine-cones where he collided with one of Gilson's men. Falling in a tangled heap, the man cursed loudly as Monty worked to extricate himself from the embarrassing collision.

Once on his feet, Monty threw a punch at the startled gunman who ducked and slammed an uppercut
into Monty's belly, knocking the wind from him. The
man scrambled about looking for his dropped gun.

Forcing himself up, Monty gulped in a lungful of
air and pushed forward, hooking both of his arms
around the man and squeezing. A volley of curses
flew from the man's lips, but Monty increased the
pressure of his bear hug.

'This is a hell of a time for you to be dancing!'

Twisting around with the gunman held tight,
Monty saw Hockman and Robeson coming toward
them. Robeson took his six-shooter and struck the
beleaguered man across the head, rattling his brain
and rendering him unconscious. Monty let the man
fall to the ground.

'Let's get over to the house,' Hochman rasped.

Before they could take another step, they were
assaulted by two men who came out of the scrub and
began firing their rifles. Miraculously, none of them
were hit, but the man Robeson had struck was just
coming to and had risen to his knees, shaking his
head. A bullet caught him on the breastbone and
rendered him lifeless.

Monty whipped his gun up and tossed a shot in
their direction as Robeson let loose with three rapid
shots from his own rifle.

A succession of gunfire snarled out from near the
corral, and Monty saw more of Gilson's men converging on the area. The men were taking up

positions near the barn and the corral which gave them good cover. Monty thought things were not going well; he was anxious for a sight of Cameron, but the Pinkerton man was nowhere to be seen. Neither were Becky and her son, for that matter, which Monty thought was a bad sign. He focused on the ranch house, but saw nothing. Briefly, he thought he heard Gilson's voice raised in anger.

Robeson ran off to the left, and disappeared into a clump of evergreen bushes.

'That damned fool is on his own!' Hockman said.

Hockman decided to sit down and fire on the corral with his rifle. He unleashed a long string of shots with practised precision, which at least sent Gilson's men scrambling for cover in the barn. With Hockman's Winchester flinging lead, those pine fence-posts became less appealing as cover with each passing moment.

Movement drew Monty's attention again to the ranch house, and he spotted Strickland dashing out and around to the rear. Monty sent a shot flying in that direction, but he was too slow. Meanwhile, Hockman had wounded one of the gunmen. He lay slumped against the corral gate holding his bloody shoulder. He was shouting to stop shooting because he was surrendering. No one paid him much attention.

The gunman that came rushing toward Monty took him by surprise. The man had appeared so quickly that Monty couldn't take a breath. Hockman turned around and blasted the man in the chest with a .45 slug that burrowed through the man's heart and obliterated it before exiting his back in a spray of crimson gore.

Some of Gilson's men had seen this and suddenly disappeared. In seconds none of Gilson's men were visible except the wounded man crumpled near the gate. Monty rose and yelled over at the man, 'Shut your mouth before I come over there and shoot you myself!'

Hockman reloaded his rifle, and with Monty at his side they made a leisurely path toward the house. It was empty, as they expected, the good news being they didn't find any bodies. Hockman said, 'I reckon Miss Drake is alive, maybe hiding.'

'If she's lucky she's with Cameron.'

'Nothing has gone the way anybody planned,' Hockman said. 'Let's mosey about and shoot some varmints as we go.'

They circled to the rear and immediately encountered trouble. A bullet chipped off a corner of the log house as Gilson's men took aim from the treeline. Hockman cursed loudly as a bullet grazed his thigh.

Monty glanced around the area, desperate for a glimpse of Cameron. Nothing, and Gilson's men seemed to have the advantage. Still, Monty wasn't fearful, not yet. Hockman and Robeson wouldn't be taken down that easily, and Cameron was still out there . . . somewhere! If he could only keep himself alive long enough to contribute to this confounded gunfight!

He was breathing heavily, which he knew was the result of a lazy life that included too much beer in the saloon and steak and potatoes whenever he had the money. Sweat dripped out from under his Stetson.

Hockman had shrugged off the grazing wound and let loose a blistering round of Winchester fire with unnerving accuracy. That man could shoot, and Gilson's men felt the brunt of that volley.

Their predicament changed when Robeson reappeared behind Gilson's men, his own rifle blazing. Hockman yelled at Robeson to keep at them as Monty decided to barrel toward one of the men who was trying to reload his rifle. The man was thumbing brass into the receiver when Monty collided with him, and once again he found himself wrestling with an *hombre* who wanted to kill him.

Exasperated, Monty clubbed the man on the head with his gun butt until the man slumped over unconscious.

Pulling himself up, Monty was beaming as Robeson and Hockman approached him from either side.

'Come on, boys!' Monty said, 'Let's find Cameron and finish off these owlhoots!'

FOURTEEN

Becky was fast. Cameron was impressed at how swiftly she moved through the woodland, and silently like an Indian. She was single-minded and determined to find her son, and Cameron couldn't help but to be impressed.

The problem they had was not knowing where Randy had gone, and Becky was surprised that they hadn't found him hiding in the forest.

'I thought for sure he'd be here,' she said. 'When he was smaller he'd hide and play up on this hill, and climb trees in the grove over there.'

'Let's think this over a minute,' Cameron offered. 'Randy is smart, but he had to think fast. Where was he when Strickland showed up?'

'He was in the house with his guitar. He left the guitar and disappeared.'

'He had to go out the back window.'

'Yes, I suppose so.'

'That's opposite this hillside. What's over in that

wooded area?'

Becky's eyes widened. 'Why, there's an old stone wall and a dried-up well.'

'A stone wall and a well?'

'There used to be a smaller farm before this one. The well dried up. All that's left are some stone walls all busted up.'

'Let's go.'

Nothing further needed to be said, and there was no place left to look. They had to come down the hill and out of the woods and cross the ranch house area to reach that location. There was no shorter route and they were burning daylight.

The gunfire from the ranch had been consistent. With their guns ready, they slipped down toward the barn. On the way across the short field of tall, swaying grass, they glimpsed Monty, Hockman and Robeson.

They reached the barn but in that instant Dave Gilson dashed from behind a wagon with a Bowie knife in his hand. He was too swift to be stopped, although Cameron had his gun on him as he knocked Becky's rifle from her hands, tugged at the locks of her hair, yanked her head back and put the knife's blade to her throat.

'You want her to live?' he hissed.

Cameron kept the rifle aimed at Gilson. 'That's not very nice of you.'

'That's all you got to say? I'm not very nice? What did you expect when you came here mister fancy boots Pinkerton man? Drop your gun or I'll kill her now!'

'All right, but don't be in such a rush. We can work this out.' Cameron lowered his gun but he didn't drop it.

'Work it out? You're crazy, that's for sure. I'm going to kill you! Now drop the gun or this woman is gonna bleed!'

Cameron nodded, 'All right, don't hurt her.' He dropped the rifle and Gilson visibly relaxed, a big greasy grin spreading across his face.

'That's more like it. I'll give you credit, Pinkerton man, you got some brass. Now it's time for you to pay for killing my brother.'

Cameron was ready. Gilson still had Becky's hair clutched in his left hand, the Bowie knife in his right, and he had moved just enough when Cameron's hand dropped to the holster on his right hip and swiftly pulled the Colt. The hammer was back and the trigger engaged in a second, but Gilson moved again as the gun barked. The bullet tore a red gash across his cheek that set him to howling.

He lunged at Cameron before he could get off another shot. Gilson locked Cameron's gun arm with his hand, twisting at the wrist and blocking his elbow to prevent him from swinging the gun around. The Bowie knife flashed at Cameron, but he followed suit by clenching his hand around Gilson's wrist. A mighty struggle proceeded, with the two men seemingly locked in a stalemate.

The sound of Becky's rifle echoed across the stable.

Gilson had a brief moment when he glanced at the stain blossoming on his shirt like an unholy rose before he fell forward, twitching his last.

Cameron took a long look at Becky. There was smoke curling from the Winchester's barrel, and that determined look had never left her face. Nor did she seem regretful in any way. She's one hell of a woman, he thought.

'Well, thanks,' he said, rubbing his chin and trying to smile nonchalantly. 'I thought for a minute I was getting a shave.'

'This is no times for jokes!' Becky retorted.

Yep, one hell of a woman, he thought, as he followed her round the barn.

The ambush had become a freewheeling series of events with both sides failing to take the advantage. Cameron recognized the lethal potential for Gilson and his remaining men to succeed, although the odds were increasingly in the lawman's favor.

Men were scattered about shooting; some on the periphery in the trees and some scrambling about the ranch house. Cameron swept his rifle around and let loose at several men dodging about the corral. His bullets didn't hit anyone but had the effect of sending the men cursing and diving for cover.

'There's Monty and the others at the doorway!' Becky said.

Cameron glanced at the ranch house where Monty was blasting away with his six-shooter. They hadn't seen Becky or him yet.

'We don't want to get caught in the crossfire,' Cameron told her. 'Let's wave at them and try to get their attention.'

'I know a faster way,' Becky responded as she levered brass into the breech. Lifting her rifle, she set her aim and shot the wall six inches to Monty's right, but low to prevent a ricochet from striking anyone inside. Monty jumped like a startled buffalo, and Becky waved her arm when he squinted in their direction.

Convening on the porch, Becky quickly asked if they had seen her son.

'No sign of him,' Monty said.

'I think I know where he might be hiding. Can you keep the house secure until we get back?'

'It might be better if we all stayed together at this point,' Robeson offered. 'We should finish these men off quickly and find Gilson.'

'Some of Gilson's men went off in that direction,' Hockman said. 'You'll need us because it's going to be a fight every step of the way.'

They proceeded toward the trees and were thirty feet away when a shot rang out and clipped Hockman in the leg. He yelped and went down, cursing.

Monty and Robeson found cover in a swell of grass as Becky let fly with several rounds from her rifle.

146

Cameron glanced back at Hockman, who had lashed his wound with a bandanna and was setting his rifle sights on the trees where the gunmen were hidden.

They made it into the trees, which gave them better cover. Now Gilson's men would be in a defensive position without being able to see Becky and Cameron. Moving as quietly as possible, they circled around and finally spotted some of Gilson's men. Cameron brought his rifle into play and his bullet cut a bloody groove across a man's cheek; the next bullet dropped him.

He spotted another man crouched near some scrub. He must have sensed Cameron was close because he turned his head and lifted his rifle; Cameron was already squinting down the barrel and pulled the trigger. The Winchester bucked and the shot plunged into the man's chest, turning him into a lifeless heap.

A burst of gunfire tore at the brush and Cameron dodged, sliding into a thicket of wildflowers and tree stumps. There was just enough cover. Becky had followed him, unperturbed, as vigilant as ever.

Crawling, they emerged on the other side of a leafy thicket, and immediately encountered two of Gilson's men. The men hadn't seen them yet. Cameron reloaded the Winchester. Then he took aim at one of them. The rifle roared and the man's head exploded. The other man saw them in that instant and scampered for cover.

The furious gun battle raged for several minutes.

Becky swept her rifle back and forth, shooting at the calculated position of Gilson's men hunkered down in the brush. It was a risk that paid off judging by the agonized screams as her bullets found their mark.

They decided to accelerate their attack, and moving side by side, they advanced into the woodland firing their guns.

One of Gilson's men came smashing through brambles waving his gun at them. Becky shot him, and paused to reload her rifle as Cameron levered his Winchester and blasted at a man who was firing at them from a thicket of birch trees. Cameron didn't have clear view of the gunman, but a few moments later they found fresh blood on the birch bark. He was wounded, and a wounded wolf was twice as dangerous.

Becky lost no time tracking him. Five minutes later they found him, and when he saw Becky approaching he spat a string of curses that would have made most women blush with embarrassment.

'If you don't throw your gun down I'm going to shoot you,' she said, sounding quite practical. Cameron almost smiled. The man cursed again and raised his gun. Becky's bullet took him in the chest. A red stain bloomed on his shirt as his knees buckled. He fell face first into the grass, his last breath gurgling in his throat.

They had little time to ponder their next action. Cameron saw another man crouching on a hillock with a rifle aimed at them. Cameron quickly shouldered his rifle, levering a round into the breech, and sighted on the man's chest. He saw the muzzle flash as the blue smoke wafted upward. The man had fired first, but had missed. His bullet whizzed in the air past them as Cameron's rifle boomed.

A succession of rifle shots took them by surprise just as they heard Gilson's voice bellowing, 'Kill them!' The gunfire stitched holes in the tree bark, showering the area with dust and splinters. Becky pulled Cameron down just as another volley ripped through the underbrush.

'Stay down!' she hissed.

They spent a few minutes scrutinizing every inch of foliage within their field of view. They didn't see Gilson, but his voice was loud and clear and not all that far away. Cameron shifted his position, sweat dripping off his face. A few seconds later he spied a second man up the trail. He took in a deep breath. Still crouching, Cameron sighted down the barrel and drew a bead on the man. The forest had become still, intruded upon only by Gilson's voice, which was trailing away. They had to move faster. His finger squeezed the trigger.

When the rifle cracked he saw a puff on the man's belly, just above his belt buckle. Then he heard the man scream as he fell.

Becky was up and running. Cameron had no choice but to leap to his feet and follow her. They ascended a steep hill, impossibly thick with pine and birch. They followed what must have been a deer trail, winding up and over until they came at last to a clearing. There was an old well here, the tattered rope and broken bucket as dry as bone. A quick survey of the area confirmed this was part of what remained of a homestead that had been abandoned long ago.

Squinting in the sunlight, he saw additional stone walls beyond the greenery where the cabin and some outlying buildings had once stood.

The place was empty.

Becky, desperate to find her son, dashed about looking for him. She cursed, which surprised Cameron.

Her gaze swept back and forth, but it was a futile effort. Randy wasn't here, and neither was Gilson. She stopped then, dropped her rifle and began weeping. Her eyes welled with tears that rolled down her cheeks. Stunned, Cameron embraced her, not sure what to say. He held her trembling body as she sobbed. That was when Strickland stepped out from behind a thick bush.

'Now isn't this a sweet sight.' His Colt was pointed at them and there was nothing Cameron could do. Although he still had his rifle in his hand, his arms were around Becky.

'Sweet like mama's apple pie, isn't that right?'

Becky stopped sobbing and he felt her body tense.

'Where's my son?'

'Gilson has the boy back there.' Strickland waved his free hand toward the crumbling walls of the old ranch visible through the trees. 'I'll give the boy some credit, he gave us all the slip, but we found him after all.'

'Give it up, Strickland. The other men will be up this way soon. You don't have a chance.'

Strickland's eyes widened with surprise. 'Give it up? You're loco, man! I'm going to kill you slowly, and then you know what I'm going to do with this woman?'

Becky forced herself free of Cameron's embrace.

'You're not going to do anything with me!' she said venomously, 'You're going to put that gun down and get away from us!'

Strickland gave out a raspy laugh. 'I'll be damned! This woman has gumption! I'm going to have fun with you, that's for sure!'

Gilson's voice drifted out from the trees. 'Bring 'em in!'

Strickland gave them a greasy smile and stepped in close, the Colt pointing at Becky's head. 'Drop that rifle or I'll kill her. Now let's go see what the boss wants to do next.'

Cameron had no choice and begrudgingly dropped his Winchester. Reacting too swiftly to be stopped, Strickland reached down and pulled Cameron's gun from his holster and tossed it away.

They were marched up the trail and slipped between the pines to find Gilson leaning against an old stone wall. Randy was tied up and sitting propped against the wall. His mouth was gagged. Gilson was wounded; a red splotch darkened his shirt. He held a Colt in his right hand. His eyes blazed malevolently at Cameron.

'I might let my son Dave skin you alive when he gets here!'

'He's dead,' Cameron said flatly.

Gilson's face darkened, his blazing eyes taking on a maniacal slant.

A long moment followed and Cameron thought Gilson would plug him right then and there. Finally, he sputtered, 'You'll feel a lot of pain before I let you die.'

'He didn't kill him,' Becky said, 'I did. So now what are you going to do? Are you going to kill me like you killed my husband?'

Becky's comment struck like a thunderbolt. Gilson stared incredulously at her. Cameron thought Gilson looked like a rattler ready to strike, his feral stare filled with more malice than a hungry, rabid wolf. Without thinking, Cameron stepped in front of Becky to shield her body. So fierce was the man's gaze that Cameron was certain he was about to shoot her in cold blood.

Strickland stepped forward to shove Cameron away, and that was when Becky decided to strike. She dove at Gilson, her fists flailing back and forth, striking him on the head and taking him by surprise.

'You son-of-a-bitch!' The words spat from her lips like a shotgun blast.

Cameron had no choice but to switch around and go for Strickland's gun. He had Strickland's wrist, his fingers digging into his flesh, when the Colt discharged. The lead blasted a hole in the dirt and Strickland tried to wrench his arm free. Cameron was stronger but the gun was held fast, its deadly, dark barrel sweeping around. If Strickland managed to thumb the hammer back, there was a real threat to Becky if that gun discharged in her direction.

Strickland was grunting from his exertions and with a mighty pull, Cameron slammed him forward and threw him off balance. Strickland went down face first, but with the gun still in his hand. Cameron pounced on his back, pummeling him with haymakers. His knuckles punched at Strickland's head, but he twisted his head so most of the blows landed on the back of his skull. He was dazed but he had enough left in him to hold onto the gun.

Cameron raised himself up somewhat and kicked Strickland in the head. His boot caught Strickland on the right jaw, and he finally let go of the gun. Cameron yanked him to his feet and immediately slammed an uppercut into his belly. With the wind knocked from his lungs, Strickland fell in a crooked heap and sat there moaning.

Cameron picked up his own gun, and he stuck Strickland's gun in his belt.

He heard voices down the trail. Monty and the other men were nearby, but still apparently engaged with some of Gilson's men.

Gilson and Randy were gone.

Becky was on the ground, moaning. Cameron

knelt down and lifted her head. The skin above her eyebrow was already swollen and turning purple. Gilson had delivered a vicious blow and then escaped. He had undoubtedly heard the other men nearby.

Becky was blinking. 'Go get Randy,' she managed to say. '*Please* go get him.'

The fight had been taken out her, but Cameron was ready. Before he could take after Gilson, Monty came rushing into the clearing huffing like a mule on a mountain trail.

'Take Becky down to the house,' Cameron told him, 'and shoot anybody that tries to stop you. I'm going after Gilson. He's got Randy.'

Monty looked at Strickland. 'Is he dead?'

'No, but I kicked him real hard. I've got his gun. Now get going.'

Monty took Becky by the arm and swung her gently around toward the trail. 'Come on, ma'am, we'll get you home.' Then looking at Cameron, Monty said, 'You stay alert! These sidewinders got a lot of venom left.'

Cameron was already pushing past the crumbling foundation and scanning the forest for a trail. He found it quickly; an old raccoon trail leading from the cabin site into the brush. There was no other way they could have gone. Cameron proceeded with his Colt in hand, but crouched low. He wasn't going to give Gilson a chance to shoot him easily. At least not before Cameron shot that evil bastard first.

There was a steady rustling sound coming from the woods ahead of him. He thought it sounded like someone struggling, and he wondered if Randy was resisting being hauled about as a prisoner. For the boy's sake, Cameron hoped he went along peacefully. Gilson was a killer; they all knew that now by the man's own admission.

Abruptly, there was a sound behind him; a boot stepped heavily on a branch, cracking it. He stopped and glanced over his shoulder. Nothing. He moved on, wary, wanting to move faster but knowing Gilson would gun him down at the first opportunity. The thought crossed his mind that Strickland was following him, even with his severe injury, but he was unarmed.

Eventually, the trail steepened and there were Gilson and Randy up ahead. Randy was struggling as Gilson tried to force him up the rocky incline.

'Give it up, Gilson!' Cameron yelled out. 'There's nowhere to go!'

In response to this, Gilson spun about and snapped off a shot in Cameron's direction. The shot was high, whizzing overhead and disappearing into the forest. The gunshot echoed dully through the woods.

Another sound behind him forced him to turn, and the movement saved his life. At first all he saw was the gleaming point of the Bowie knife slashing toward his head, and he dodged as it cut the air less than an inch from his head. If he hadn't moved, the knife would have caught the jugular vein in his neck, and that would have finished him.

Strickland was raging like a rabid wolf, his lips spewing spittle and his bloodshot eyes blazing with hatred. If Cameron didn't know better, he would have sworn the man was crazed, caught up in a fever he couldn't control. In a way he was, possessed by a deep evil and hatred that Cameron had underestimated. Strickland wanted him dead, and one way or another that Bowie knife would find flesh.

Cameron kicked him, pushed him back. That slowed him, but it didn't stop him. Cameron fired once, the bullet taking Strickland high on the right side of his chest. Cameron had a glimpse of the red gore that spewed from the exit wound in Strickland's back. Strickland's lips were moving, but the sounds he made were not any language. Drool and spit flew from his lips, and then blood. He dropped the Bowie knife as his legs gave out, and he fell on one knee, tottered a moment and then fell face first into the dirt as a gout of blood burst from his nostrils. He twitched and then stopped moving.

Enough time had been wasted. Cameron had turned, ready to fire on Gilson. Instead, he lowered his gun. Gilson was being kicked by Randy, and although the boy had his mouth gagged and his wrists lashed with rope, he had managed to kick Gilson between the legs. In his weakened state, Gilson was in no condition to withstand the onslaught of a hard boot repeatedly kicking his lower extremities.

Cameron approached, still concerned about the gun held in Gilson's feeble hand. When Gilson's eyes fell on Cameron, he seemed revitalized by his anger and tried to stand up and aim his gun. Cameron stepped in quickly and swept his gun hard across Gilson's head, tearing a bloody gash in his skull and knocking him senseless.

'That's enough out of you,' Cameron said. 'You're going to jail.'

EPILOGUE

Sheriff Charlie Kerrigan recovered from his wound and saw to it that Jim Gilson stood trial for murder and robbery in Hays City. Gilson was found guilty, and had recovered from his own wounds sufficiently before they hanged him. Sheriff Kerrigan had argued with the judge that Gilson was extremely dangerous and should be hanged immediately, but the judge stated that would constitute cruel and unusual punishment, so Gilson was held in jail under a doctor's care. A full six weeks passed before they hanged him.

Monty, Hockman and Robeson were written up in the newspaper as local heroes. Cameron was mentioned as a contributor to their success and referred to as a 'special representative of the Pinkerton Detective Agency', which was factual. Sheriff Kerrigan personally thanked Cameron for his role in bringing Gilson to justice, and then told him to get out of town.

'Now, sheriff, that's real unfriendly of you,' Cameron said. 'The fact is I'm hiring on at the Drake ranch. Becky has asked me to help out and I'm a bit tired of chasing outlaws. I hope to see you around.'

Cameron sent a formal letter of resignation to Alan Pinkerton, who responded with a gracious personal note thanking him for his service.

He hadn't said as much to anyone, but Cameron had known for some time that staying close to Becky Drake was exactly the right thing to do. He had already started writing a new song, and one day soon he'd play it for her.

We'll be happy at Skyline Ranch
Where the apples are on the branch;
Where the trail of my life
Has brought me a fine wife,
And the jingle of my spurs
Means I'm riding to see her;
And this here lonely trail
Tells the ending of my tale.

Life on the farm offered country comfort and hard work, and that was all he needed. For too long he had been surrounded by gunfire. Back at Skyline Ranch it was as if nature resumed its course following all of this turmoil. The small birds that were so common around the farm had returned now that the gunfire had ceased. The big brown speckled cattle grazed in the field, and the late afternoon light was golden and tranquil. The skyline was absent of riders. Cameron went about his chores punctually and earnestly, content at last that he might have accomplished something of value. There was no reason to hurry. No reason at all. Time was like a river that carried them all to their fate, he thought, and here he was; and Becky was a soft yet vibrant presence that filled him with hope. They both understood when they looked at each other, although neither of them had mentioned it yet, that the hired hand's cot in the bunkhouse was only temporary.